An instant before the man moved, Bolan anticipated his action

The Executioner instinctively jerked his head to one side as the man's fist jabbed the air, passing a hair's width from his face. With the breeze from the missed blow caressing his cheek, Bolan took a quick step forward, driving a handful of stiff fingers into his attacker's throat. The man coughed and clutched at his neck with both hands, stumbling back a few feet. His legs buckled and he fell to one knee, fighting to suck in air.

Before the man's partner could react, Bolan unleashed a rapid flurry of short punches to his face. The man attempted to strike back, but he was falling away from the volley, his momentum pulling him in the wrong direction. His return jabs landed harmlessly on Bolan's muscular forearms.

The warrior stepped back to place a little distance between them. His victim staggered, breathing raggedly. As he spat a thick glob of bloody phlegm toward Bolan, he reached into his pocket and pulled out a switchblade. He didn't know it, but he was about to learn a lesson in arms proliferation—escalation always leads to greater violence.

MACK BOLAN ®

The Executioner

#281 Blood Stone
#282 Jungle Conflict
#283 Ring of Retaliation
#284 Devil's Army
#285 Final Strike
#286 Armageddon Exit
#287 Rogue Warrior
#288 Arctic Blast
#289 Vendetta Force
#290 Pursued
#291 Blood Trade
#292 Savage Game
#293 Death Merchants
#294 Scorpion Rising
#295 Hostile Alliance
#296 Nuclear Game
#297 Deadly Pursuit
#298 Final Play
#299 Dangerous Encounter
#300 Warrior's Requiem
#301 Blast Radius
#302 Shadow Search
#303 Sea of Terror
#304 Soviet Specter
#305 Point Position
#306 Mercy Mission
#307 Hard Pursuit
#308 Into the Fire
#309 Flames of Fury
#310 Killing Heat
#311 Night of the Knives
#312 Death Gamble
#313 Lockdown
#314 Lethal Payload
#315 Agent of Peril
#316 Poison Justice
#317 Hour of Judgment
#318 Code of Resistance

#319 Entry Point
#320 Exit Code
#321 Suicide Highway
#322 Time Bomb
#323 Soft Target
#324 Terminal Zone
#325 Edge of Hell
#326 Blood Tide
#327 Serpent's Lair
#328 Triangle of Terror
#329 Hostile Crossing
#330 Dual Action
#331 Assault Force
#332 Slaughter House
#333 Aftershock
#334 Jungle Justice
#335 Blood Vector
#336 Homeland Terror
#337 Tropic Blast
#338 Nuclear Reaction
#339 Deadly Contact
#340 Splinter Cell
#341 Rebel Force
#342 Double Play
#343 Border War
#344 Primal Law
#345 Orange Alert
#346 Vigilante Run
#347 Dragon's Den
#348 Carnage Code
#349 Firestorm
#350 Volatile Agent
#351 Hell Night
#352 Killing Trade
#353 Black Death Reprise
#354 Ambush Force
#355 Outback Assault
#356 Defense Breach

The Executioner
Don Pendleton's®
DEFENSE BREACH

A GOLD EAGLE BOOK FROM

W🌐RLDWIDE®

TORONTO • NEW YORK • LONDON
AMSTERDAM • PARIS • SYDNEY • HAMBURG
STOCKHOLM • ATHENS • TOKYO • MILAN
MADRID • WARSAW • BUDAPEST • AUCKLAND

First edition July 2008

ISBN-13: 978-0-373-64356-1
ISBN-10:   0-373-64356-X

Special thanks and acknowledgment to
Peter Spring for his contribution to this work.

DEFENSE BREACH

Never yield to force; never yield to the apparently overwhelming might of the enemy.

—Sir Winston Churchill,
1874–1965

The odds might be against me and my enemies outnumber me, but that will never stop me from executing my plan of attack.

—Mack Bolan

THE
MACK BOLAN

LEGEND

Nothing less than a war could have fashioned the destiny of the man called Mack Bolan. Bolan earned the Executioner title in the jungle hell of Vietnam.

But this soldier also wore another name—Sergeant Mercy. He was so tagged because of the compassion he showed to wounded comrades-in-arms and Vietnamese civilians.

Mack Bolan's second tour of duty ended prematurely when he was given emergency leave to return home and bury his family, victims of the Mob. Then he declared a one-man war against the Mafia.

He confronted the Families head-on from coast to coast, and soon a hope of victory began to appear. But Bolan had broken society's every rule. That same society started gunning for this elusive warrior—to no avail.

So Bolan was offered amnesty to work within the system against terrorism. This time, as an employee of Uncle Sam, Bolan became Colonel John Phoenix. With a command center at Stony Man Farm in Virginia, he and his new allies—Able Team and Phoenix Force—waged relentless war on a new adversary: the KGB.

But when his one true love, April Rose, died at the hands of the Soviet terror machine, Bolan severed all ties with Establishment authority.

Now, after a lengthy lone-wolf struggle and much soul-searching, the Executioner has agreed to enter an "arm's-length" alliance with his government once more, reserving the right to pursue personal missions in his Everlasting War.

1

Mack Bolan pressed the motor's throttle, and his snow-mobile sped over the snow-crusted prairie. Cold air sneaking around the lenses of his goggles caused his eyes to water. He leaned into the sleek machine's composite frame as frozen terrain raced by inches below his boots.

Sound carried a long way across the open plains of Manitoba where, at this time of year, the crystal clear air was as frigid as arctic ice. But he wasn't worried about noise from his CIA-developed snowmobile announcing its approach. Canada's immense wilderness immediately swallowed the barely audible hum produced by the vehicle's power pack. The energy unit was an engineering marvel—small enough to fit under the snowmobile's seat while still providing the needed muscle to leap from zero to sixty miles per hour in under ten seconds.

If his presence was discovered ahead of time, Bolan thought it would be via the radar technology Akira Tokaido had briefed him about back at Stony Man Farm. Displaying a determined stealth born in the jungles of Southeast Asia and tempered on hellfire trails around the world, the man some knew as the Executioner all but flew over the packed snow at breakneck speed, a fleeting blur against a monochrome landscape.

Bolan was dressed entirely in white, from the lined face mask with attached skull cap covering his black hair, to the white Corcoran Jump Boots stitched onto nonskid soles embedded with diamond dust to ensure gripping stability on ice. His formfitting parka and snow pants were fabricated from an extremely thin and pliable synthetic blend. The resulting tight cross weave produced a silky fabric that would keep him comfortable at temperatures down to minus thirty degrees Fahrenheit. Equally important, Bolan's attire provided warmth without a trace of bulkiness or binding that might restrict life-preserving arm and leg movements. As if to test his clothing's response, he locked his elbows and straightened his muscular torso, stretching his spine for a few moments before settling back down behind the snowmobile's white fuselage.

Over the eye cutouts in his face mask, Bolan wore nonreflective polycarbonate goggles set in white frames with large wraparound sides. He knew it was essential to avoid the condition alpine skiers referred to as snow blindness. In his line of work, a case of snow blindness during a mission was as much a fatal condition as inoperable lung cancer.

A quick glance at the dashboard clock's LED told him he was on schedule to reach his destination before dark in spite of the fact that the winter sun, hurried by the season's extended nights, had already passed its zenith and continued to march steadily toward the western horizon. As he maintained a course due north, the crouched shadow keeping pace on the snow beside him seemed to grow taller by the minute, serving as a steady reminder of the daylight's unremitting flight.

Based on the intel provided to him, it was important that Bolan reach the cabin before nightfall. As it was, he knew he might already be too late to stop the transfer of a top secret computer code to a terrorist group in the Middle East. According to Hal Brognola, director of the Justice Department's Sensitive Operations Group, the code would enable them to successfully attack a United States aircraft carrier, killing thousands of Navy personnel. Determined to prevent that, Bolan pushed on.

When he was approximately one hour south of his objective, he again recalled the conversation with Hal Brognola two days earlier in the shade of the Washington Monument that had brought him three hundred miles into Canada for his reconnaissance mission.

At that meeting, Brognola's breath had punctuated his words with little white clouds as he spoke. "As commander in chief, the President has a sacred obligation to protect the American soldiers and sailors under his authority," Brognola said while they walked west along the National Mall with the Capitol Building at their backs. "His words, not mine."

"What's the worst-case scenario?" Bolan asked.

Brognola turned up his overcoat's collar against the icy breeze that was blowing off the Potomac River and exhaled before answering, his breath appearing in a steady plume as thick as cigar smoke. "The Navy's aircraft carriers are protected with a system called ADAS—Air Defense Alert System—designed and built by Nautech Corporation," Brognola replied. "Worst-case scenario would be a terrorist group getting access to the computer code that gives ADAS its instructions. If an enemy was able to communicate with the program installed onboard a ship, hidden commands could be inserted into the operating system instructing ADAS to drop its electronic sensors. If that happened, our aircraft carriers would be like fish in a barrel."

"How does the system work?" the Executioner asked.

The big Fed squinted into the distance for a moment before replying. He was wearing a charcoal gray topcoat that came to his knees, and a black felt fedora whose narrow brim cast the upper half of his face in shadow. A silk scarf printed with a rose-and-maroon paisley pattern filled the space between the topcoat's wool collar and Brognola's neck. In spite of the snow, his black wingtips were clean and shiny, his appearance as impeccable as if he had just come from a Fortune 500 boardroom.

Still looking toward a distant horizon, he said, "When the ADAS cabinets are deployed onboard aircraft carriers, twenty-seven monitors that resemble small television screens are also installed and connected to the system. The monitors are mounted in various places—some on the bridge, in the weapons center, one in the captain's quarters, some in the mess hall. The point is to put them all over the ship to make sure that both the captain and the weapons officer will always be close to one. The system grabs real-time electronic information from the ship's radar and weapons systems, and displays everything approaching the vessel within thirty nautical miles. ADAS also keeps track of available weapons and missile inventories, automatically matching incoming targets with the appropriate weapons to neutralize them."

"Like a big video game," Bolan commented.

"Except that life and death are at stake," Brognola replied dryly. "Today's weapons systems are able to assess the environment, make decisions and initiate action within seconds. You don't have much time to figure out the best course of action when a few warheads are speeding toward your ship at Mach 2. ADAS does it all in split seconds. Recognizes the targets, assigns weapons, tracks, engages, mitigates. The USS *Stark* taught the Navy what happens when you don't have an electronic umbrella monitoring your immediate area for incoming threats."

Brognola adjusted his scarf with an efficient motion that suggested the gentle tugging and tucking might be a habit rather than a necessity. "If a terrorist group got their hands on Nautech's top secret computer codes running ADAS," he said, directing his gaze at Bolan, "they could blind our ships to incoming missiles. There are two or three aircraft carriers stationed in the Persian Gulf at any given time. Each one is a floating arsenal, transporting unbelievable weaponry to the modern-day battlefield. Fighter jets, bombers, guns, missiles—these nuclear-powered vessels are true death stars. They also cost close to a billion dollars to build and maintain. Losing even one in combat would be devastating. And not just because of the cost. Aircraft carriers represent the epitome of American military might. It would be a serious blow to both troop morale and our global prestige if we lost a carrier."

Brognola sighed heavily. "We need a soft probe, Striker. I can't give you all the details here, but the objective is in Manitoba, about three hundred miles from the North Dakota border. We think a group of engineers from Nautech have hijacked the computer code and are planning to sell it on the black market."

Bolan finished reading the four-page briefing Homeland Security had given the President earlier that morning and passed it back to Brognola. The edges of the papers ruffled in the breeze as the big Fed folded the report before slipping it into his overcoat's internal breast pocket and buttoning the flap closed.

Bolan recalled missions he had accomplished in part

aboard aircraft carriers, remembering the highly charged atmosphere where a crew of up to five thousand dedicated men and women worked in harmony to bring the enormous might of their vessel to bear. Brognola was right. It would be significant on a number of levels for the United States to lose a national asset like an aircraft carrier.

Soft probe, Bolan thought. How many times had he heard the words "soft," "cold," or "unoccupied" used to incorrectly describe one of his drop zones? For Brognola to be requesting his assistance, the situation had to have already progressed to a point where the President no longer trusted his official people to mitigate the threat before it affected policy.

"Okay," Bolan said suddenly.

"Akira's ready to brief you," Brognola responded, referring to the talented hacker who served on Aaron "The Bear" Kurtzman's cybernetics team at Stony Man Farm.

The two men parted without another word, the man from the Justice Department setting off to inform the President that his request had been accepted; the man known to Brognola as "Striker" stepping away and turning up Twelfth Street. By the time the warrior had passed between the EPA and IRS buildings, he had merged with the few pedestrians braving the January cold, vanishing into the cityscape as effectively as a tiger disappeared into the jungle. The rules for survival were, if fact, the same everywhere.

An alarm sounded on the snowmobile's dashboard. The electronic unit was alerting Bolan that he was entering an area being scanned by the type of radiation used to power long-distance surveillance radars. He brought his snowmobile to a halt and turned off the sensor.

In the stillness, he could hear snowmobiles. They

were far away, at least three or four miles, the distance making it impossible to discern whether they were heading his way. Bolan's experience on battlefields throughout the world had developed in him a phenomenal sense of space and distance. It was no coincidence that ancient cultures often portrayed their legendary warriors with ears resembling those of bats. In hand-to-hand combat, extraordinary fighters sometimes displayed an intimate feel for their surroundings so extreme they appeared to be operating with the assistance of a sixth sonarlike sense. Bolan listened hard for a few seconds before deciding the snowmobiles were moving away from his position.

He switched the sensor back on. The intermittent chirping pattern signified he was at the extreme edge of coverage. On the unit's LED, the scanning frequency was identified as one residing at the long end of the L-band, verifying Tokaido's assertion that the engineers from Nautech would probably use energy bands similar to those they worked with at the company. The radiation's magnitude, however, was of more interest to Bolan than its actual frequency. By measuring the intensity of the beam sweeping across the open plain, Tokaido's sensor was able to get a lock on the source's location. According to the display, the cabin was roughly five miles away, which meant Bolan had probably not shown up yet on their screen. Before resuming his approach, he turned on his unit's cloaking circuit.

"It's only a snowmobile," Akira Tokaido had replied to Barbara Price's compliment after the hacker showed Stony Man Farm's mission controller that there were methods other than physical design to shield items from radar detection. "It's not like we're hiding a battleship or anything."

Well-known weapons such as the American Stealth bomber and South Korea's KDX-II destroyer used angles and composite coatings to deflect or absorb radar transmissions. Tokaido, however, knew how to use electronic tweaking, what he referred to as "turning a mirror on the illuminator," to shield almost anything from conventional radars.

With the unit's LED emitting a steady green light indicating that an electronic cloak had been wrapped around him and his snowmobile, Bolan resumed his advance. It was growing colder, causing his exhaled breath to immediately form into ice crystals on the outside of his face mask. He pressed on, oblivious to the cold.

Bolan heard the generator a good ten minutes before the cabin came into sight. The sun was slightly less than an hour from setting when he halted his snowmobile and dismounted in one of the waist-deep gullies that pocked the plain. The snow formations in this area resembled shallow riverbeds, the shapes blown into the prairie in much the same way water sculpted a stream's dirt banks. After performing a quick touch-check on the weapons he wore, Bolan crawled to the edge of the snow brim where he could see the outline of the cabin tucked into the edge of a small stand of spruce bordering a sparse coppice of hardwood and pine.

A bone-chilling wind from the north fueled to life more than a dozen miniature tornadoes of fine dry snow, setting them swirling wildly in front of Bolan's position. The whirlwinds danced for minutes at a time across his field of vision before each fell abruptly back to earth, only to be instantly replaced by others leaping skyward from the white powder.

Distances were deceiving on a flat terrain where the sun, while low on the horizon, was nevertheless still brilliant. Even coming in at an extreme angle, rays shining onto a pristine white countryside devoid of color often played tricks. Bolan scanned the area before him in long overlapping sweeps, estimating the cabin to be slightly more than a half mile away. The building was cast in late-afternoon shadow by half a dozen spruce trees whose gnarled and misshapen boughs were testimony to the number of years they had stood like sentries, their crooked growth influenced by decade after decade of the wind's unrelenting push.

Bolan reached into one of the pouches on his white combat belt and withdrew a pair of binoculars whose lenses were composed of the same material he wore in his goggles. The compact binoculars were ruggedized, which meant they could withstand harsh environments, including shock and vibration, without a resultant performance loss. Bolan peered through the eyecups while fingering the focus wheel.

Despite the generator's noise, the cabin appeared to be deserted, but three snowmobiles pulled into a tight huddle against the building's east wall belied the initial impression. Bolan switched the binoculars into infrared mode, causing the landscape to shimmer for a few seconds while the internal photocathode sensors adjusted to the IR data stream. Processed from a half mile away, an infrared view's validity was suspect, but the image coming through the lenses clearly showed that the cabin walls were considerably warmer than its surroundings. The snowmobiles emitted a color profile that indicated none of the engines had been fired up recently. Notwithstanding the apparent inactivity, Bolan would approach the cabin as if the people inside were armed and awaiting his arrival.

He lowered the binoculars and put them back into

their pouch. As he pushed himself away from the berm's shallow lip, he took mental inventory of his weapons.

In a white leather holster riding low on his hip, the soldier wore a .44-caliber Desert Eagle. If called into service, the oversize handgun's appetite would be fed with the two hundred rounds of Cor-Bon 249-grain ammo he carried in one of the pouches on his white combat belt.

Bolan's Beretta 93-R, loaded with a 20-round clip of 9 mm Parabellum ammunition, was housed in a shoulder holster with Velcro flap. In one of the pouches on his combat belt, Bolan carried two hundred additional 9 mm rounds and the pistol's sound suppressor. This mission did not overtly call for a suppressor, but after spending a good portion of his life in conditions that wavered to the whims of battle uncertainty, Bolan knew there was no such thing as being too prepared or too well-equipped for a job.

A foot-long Sykes-Fairbairn tempered steel knife, honed to a razor's edge, rested in a white leather sheath strapped to the outside of his right calf. Four MK3A2 concussion grenades hooked to the combat belt's webbing ensured the availability of additional firepower in the event his planned soft probe took an unexpectedly intense turn.

Bolan climbed back onto his snowmobile, started the motor and circled around to the cabin's far side. Numerous tracks in the snow close to the building alerted him that there had been recent visitors. Although not as unique as tire tracks, the traces on the ground displayed sufficient variation for Bolan to determine that four separate snowmobiles had arrived from the west, departing in the same direction. He eased his vehicle into the cover of the thin woods behind the cabin, cruising twenty yards among the trees until he found a spot affording acceptable concealment. Once there, he switched off the motor. As he dismounted and drew his Beretta, a crow cried out from its perch in a nearby tree, and the warrior paused to listen to nature's voice. The very distant drone of the snowmobiles he had registered earlier was the only man-made sound reaching his ears.

On feet as silent as those of a stalking tiger, he swiftly covered the distance between the cabin and woods. Reaching the structure, he pressed himself against the weathered siding close to where a propane gas tank was mounted on a steel frame. There was no sound from within. Before entering, he removed his protective goggles and put them away, exposing blue eyes that darted from one point to another, continuously processing information relative to his surroundings.

Bolan inched closer to the door, raising his Beretta to the ready position. When he reached the doorknob, he halted for a second, steeling himself for whatever he might find inside. Knowing he might come under gunfire as soon as his presence was discovered, he took hold of the doorknob and turned, finding it unlocked. Without further delay, he stepped into the cabin where the nauseating stench of death immediately accosted his nostrils.

With dusk settling over the region, the light inside was dim, coming from a single overhead bulb hanging from an extension cord stapled to the ceiling. The cabin was built with three rooms, the austerity of furnishings bearing testament to its short-term use. An open area contained a beat-up table and half a dozen chairs arranged in the vicinity of a propane stove. A tiny bathroom with a stall shower visible through an open door was situated against the rear wall and a bedroom with an open curtain in place of a door was next to the bathroom. On the floor in the center of the main room, two bullet-ridden bodies lay in grotesque death poses, their blood mingling on the floorboards in an irregular dark stain occupying the space between them. One of the corpses had been shot numerous times—some bullets obviously postmortem, as if the purpose of the additional slugs was to eradicate the victim's identity. Indeed, identifying the disfigured corpse based on facial evidence alone would be impossible. Why, Bolan wondered, weren't they both mutilated?

With pistol drawn, he made his way silently to the back bedroom, taking care to avoid stepping in the bloodstains splattered randomly across the floor. There should have been electronic equipment here—at the very least, a radiation source and monitoring device. If the radar Tokaido's module had detected was not coming from this cabin, where was its origin? There were no other possibilities.

The bedroom was considerably darker than the outer room. Bolan pulled a powerful pen flashlight from one of his pouches and swept the interior with its beam, his eyes scanning the space before him while he listened for signs of life. In the seam where the floorboards met the distant wall, the flashlight's beam played across a line of bright yellow sawdust, the color alerting him to the fact that the dust had not been there for a full winter during which time the elements would have turned it an oxidized gray.

Recalling the three snowmobiles outside, Bolan stepped into the center of the room and pushed the bed against a wall. The outline of a trapdoor was visible in the floorboards, a rectangle approximately three feet by two. Whoever constructed the door had done a good job placing the hinges on the underside; with only a casual glance under the bed to make sure no one was hiding there, the door would have gone unnoticed.

"Police!" he shouted to alert whomever might be under the floorboards. He had told lies much worse than impersonating an officer of the law. "Come out with your hands up."

There was no response.

Bolan placed the penlight between his teeth and drew his knife, sliding the blade into the crack forming one of the short sides. Using the weapon as a lever, he discovered there was no locking mechanism on the door. With minimal effort he was able to pry it open a few inches, which then grew wider as he pushed down on the knife's leather grip. When there was sufficient space between the door and the floor, he grabbed the hatch's edge with the hand holding his Beretta and threw it back all the way. The door banged open onto the floorboards, sounding unnaturally loud in the still of the bedroom.

"Please! Please don't kill me," came from the darkness below. The words were spoken in a voice laced with terror.

Bolan had been exposed to people on the brink of hysteria innumerable times throughout his career, and it was never a situation he preferred. Survival in his line of work was often dependent on controlling more variables than his opponent, and people scared out of their wits were not easy to control. He turned sideways to reduce his profile and held the penlight away from his body as he shone the beam into the void.

A woman was huddled in the far corner, her eyes blinking in rapid response to the light.

"Please," she said in a vacant voice.

"I won't hurt you," Bolan replied, holstering his Beretta upon seeing she was alone and unarmed.

"I thought you were one of them. They're coming back," she stated.

The dugout was about four feet deep and tiny, cramped by a single electronics cabinet that hummed evenly next to a small table supporting a computer monitor. A pair of industrial-gauge wires ran from the cabinet to the monitor, on which Bolan could see six incandescent green blips moving in a tight group.

"Does that tell you how far away they are?" he asked.

Her eyes wandered to the screen where they rested for a moment before she shook her head and repeated vacuously, "They're coming back."

"Come on," the Executioner said.

The woman pushed herself away from the wall and grabbed Bolan's outstretched hand to boost herself out of the dugout and onto the bedroom floor. As Bolan pulled her to her feet, he gave her an appraising look while slipping the penlight back into its pouch.

She was disheveled and dirty, dressed in jeans and an unzipped maroon ski parka over a gray sweatshirt with *San Diego Chargers* emblazoned in cursive pink across the front. Bolan guessed she was in her late twenties. The earrings she wore, along with the stylish cut of her jet-black hair, told him she was neither a camper nor a survivalist.

"Don't look," Bolan said as he led her out of the bedroom toward the cabin's door.

"I heard." Her voice caught in her throat and her knees buckled, causing her to lean in to Bolan. He put his arm around her, supporting her weight until they came to the door. "They kept shooting Davey," she said. "They kept shooting him, but Wes couldn't give them what they wanted. I was afraid he was going to tell them where I was hiding. They kept asking if there were three of us."

"What did they want from Wes?" Bolan asked.

She sniffed once before her eyes began spilling tears as if an inner dam had suddenly given way. "The rest of the code!" she said in a hitching voice that shook her entire body. "Wes only had half. After they left I kept trying to call 911 on my cell phone. I couldn't get through to…" Her voice tapered off.

"Do you work for Nautech?" Bolan asked.

"We all do."

"What's your name?"

She swallowed hard and wiped her tear-streaked cheeks with her palms before replying, "Sherry Krautzer."

"Okay, Sherry. We're getting out of here."

Winter darkness fell quickly in Manitoba. When Bolan pushed the cabin door open, he discovered it was as black as midnight outside. He grabbed Sherry's hand and started pulling her toward the spot in the woods where his equipment was stashed, realizing before they took half a dozen steps that the snowmobiles he had heard earlier were much closer now.

"Hurry," he said. "You have to hide in the woods until I take care of them. Understand?"

Her teeth were chattering when she replied, "Marlene said no one would get hurt. But they kept shooting Davey to make Wes tell them. Wes doesn't know who has the other half. None of us do."

Bolan jerked her arm roughly, realizing she was going into shock.

"Listen," he said, pulling her to within inches of his face when they reached the tree line. "If they see you, they'll kill you. Do you understand me? You have to stay hidden."

She was nodding when he pushed her to the ground under the canopy of a sprawling pine where she wouldn't be spotted.

"Don't move until I come to get you. Understand?"

She nodded again, but the way she kept touching her face with fluttering hands and looking about with vacant eyes did little to reassure Bolan, who understood from experience the unpredictability extreme terror caused.

"Sherry. Do not move until I come get you. They're coming back to kill you," he said.

"Okay." She paused, then repeated, "Okay."

Bolan left her concealed behind the pine boughs and ran to find a position offering sufficient cover from automatic weapons. Before killing Wes, they had apparently made him watch while they mutilated his friend's corpse. The fact that they had taken a psychological rather than physical approach to torture was telling. They were either thugs receiving specific instructions from a handler who kept them under tight control, or they were well-trained, intelligent operatives with authority to ad lib. Fanatical terrorists blindly following orders were one thing—skilled professional soldiers dedicated to a greater cause were an entirely different matter. When survival was at stake, Bolan preferred going up against the former.

The snowmobiles appeared in his binoculars as six specks of light when they were still miles from the section where trees grew in shallow stands dotting the open prairie. Sherry said that Davey and Wes were able to give their killers only one-half of the code. Bolan thought amateurs might naively believe they were protected when dealing with terrorist elements by not turning over the complete package until they received full payment. But what an inexperienced person might not understand was a terrorist's willingness to torture and steal rather than part with money that could be better spent on recruitment, weapons and training.

They'd kill everyone involved simply to cover their
tracks and eliminate all traces of their transactions.
Bolan had witnessed the scenario too many times to
count. In a transaction pitting rookies against professionals, the pros always won.

As he watched the approaching snowmobile headlights, he pondered the group's return. Sherry had tried
to make a call on her cell phone, not realizing that out here
in the wilderness, the probability of being in range of a
communications tower was slim. What she had actually
done was send out an electronic ping that announced
her presence while it searched for a connection. The
killers had to have picked up the transmission on a
scanner and realized that the third person they suspected could have been with Davey and Wes was, in fact,
in the cabin. They were coming back to finish the job.

They were about to get more than they bargained for,
the Executioner thought.

From his position at the base of a thick maple, Bolan
reached into the pouch on his web belt containing his
night-vision goggles. He focused the goggles, bringing
the six pinpoints of light into sharp relief. Magnified
hundreds of times as they passed through the internal
photocathode tube, the photons from the approaching
headlights shone with the intensity of search beacons.
Each snowmobile carried a single rider, and it appeared
that one vehicle was pulling a sled holding something
that resembled a miniature howitzer. From its profile,
Bolan was sure the item was a weapon of some type. Its
pertinent characteristics, he knew, would soon become
known. He drew his Beretta 93-R from its shoulder
holster, reached into the pouch holding the handgun's
suppressor and screwed the extension onto the end of
the pistol's barrel. He knew there was going to be

gunfire, and figured he should delay announcing his location until absolutely necessary.

The snowmobiles maintained a steady speed, splitting up when they came close. The vehicle pulling the sled with the unknown weapon halted approximately twenty yards from the cabin, while two veered off toward Bolan and the other three set out to circle the structure and cruise along the adjacent tree line from the opposite direction. The precision of their maneuver reinforced Bolan's earlier consideration that they might be skilled combatants. He remained silent as the pair coming his way passed in front of his position, taking note of their weapons as they passed.

The men were armed with Uzi submachine guns slung across their chests on canvas slings. The fixed wooden stocks were characteristic of the very early versions of the famous weapon, but Bolan knew enough not to assume that the vintage models were anything less than lethal.

Through his night-vision goggles, Bolan studied the man with the sled weapon as he began preparing the contraption. At first glance it appeared to be a stubby cylinder mounted onto a rectangular metal box, but as Bolan continued to observe, he noted that the tube was not hollow, and thick cables ran the entire length of the protrusion. There was a sighting mechanism close to one end, and dual handles similar to those found on antiaircraft guns. The operator fiddled with what had to have been dials or switches on his side of the box before grasping the dual handles and maneuvering the tube. The comparison to an antiaircraft gun was further reinforced with the cylinder being mounted on a free-floating ball pedestal affording the gunner complete three-axis rotation.

The two men who had passed Bolan continued on their slow route circling the cabin. They were halfway between Bolan and Sherry's hiding place when she abruptly burst from under the pine, hysterically begging them not to kill her. As they hastily grabbed to pull their Uzis into firing position, Bolan's silenced 93-R coughed twice in such rapid succession the rounds sounded as if they shared a single retort.

The first 9 mm Parabellum round struck the driver of the snowmobile on Bolan's right, entering the base of his neck on an upward trajectory. The hot lead tore through his skull, exiting from the center of his forehead and splattering most of his frontal lobes onto the machine's dashboard controls. The tissue immediately froze upon contact with cold metal that had been exposed to frigid air for hours. The man's throttle hand froze in a death grip, causing his snowmobile to surge forward, accelerating him directly into the side of the building where the machine crashed and revved angrily while the spinning tread underneath chewed and spit out a thin stream of snow for a few seconds before stalling.

His partner fared no better. Bolan's second bullet slammed a millisecond after the first into the middle of his back, piercing his heart and shattering his sternum on its way out. The gaping chest wound left in the slug's wake was immediately filled with a scarlet fountain rushing forth in a torrent of steaming blood that painted a thick swath across the ground. He slumped forward, bounced off the steering wheel and fell sideways into the snow. His vehicle came to an abrupt stop a few feet from the lifeless body.

The mind-numbing chatter of automatic fire filled the air as the three who had circled the cabin from the other direction opened fire on Sherry. The 9 mm steel-jacketed rounds sliced diagonally from her left knee to her right shoulder, causing the young woman to jerk and dance wildly. A burst into her upper torso lifted her off her feet and hammered her backward into the woods, where she landed faceup, unseeing eyes staring into the star-studded sky.

Realizing they were under attack, the gunmen immediately shifted their fire away from the dead woman and began hosing the woods with a steady stream of lethal lead. Not being sure of Bolan's position, they swept their weapons in wide overlapping arcs, reducing branches and saplings to a blizzard of matchsticks that rained down onto their intended victim's head.

With their wild response telling him that his enemies had not yet zeroed in on his position, Bolan remained prone while pulling the Desert Eagle off his hip.

An electronic humming, so low it sounded almost like an earthquake's rumbling, emanated from the sled weapon. The operator shouted out a warning to his companions seconds before the hum increased in both intensity and pitch. The entire cabin began to vibrate. Thin tendrils of smoke rose from the weathered siding like surface fog rolling across a body of water, then the cabin abruptly burst into flame. An instant later, the propane tank exploded in a fireball reaching two hundred feet into the sky.

Microwave, Bolan thought, immediately elevating the weapon's operator to the top of his hit list. Unaware that his cohorts on the other side of the cabin were under attack, the gunner leaned forward over a control panel to make an adjustment, exposing the upper half of his body. With the noise from the crackling fire racing through the wooden structure masking his Desert Eagle's authoritative discharge, Bolan squeezed off a single round while remaining concealed behind the base of the thick maple. The pistol's hefty .44-caliber slug caught the microwave gunner square in his chest, tossing him airborne for a few seconds. He bounced once upon hitting the frozen ground, landing on his back with arms extended to the sides.

The Executioner directed his fire toward one of the remaining three who was visible beyond the burning cabin. Pulling the trigger as rapidly as he could, he released a stream of bullets, forcing the gunman within his line of sight to dive off his snowmobile and take cover behind the vehicle. Bolan's rounds sparked and whined as they impacted the snowmobile's metal fuselage, adding to the visual and auditory chaos of combat.

Displaying a telling level of advanced training, the gunmen fanned out in an attempt to separate sufficiently to establish a triangular focus on Bolan's position, which was now fully exposed by the Desert Eagle's prolonged volley. While the two who were still mounted on snowmobiles moved away, the man on the ground covered their progress with his Uzi on full-auto, filling the air around Bolan with deadly shot.

The warrior had seen the maneuver countless times. If he stayed put, his enemies would flank his position and kill him in a cross fire. He remained low while edging away from the tree trunk, waiting for a break when the gunman would be changing magazines. As if his enemy was enacting his mental script, there was a momentary tapering off in the covering fire, and Bolan seized the opportunity to dash in a crouch into the thin woods to the spot ten yards away where he had stashed his snowmobile. As he ran, he ejected the spent magazine in his Desert Eagle, grabbed into his ammo pouch for a fresh one and rammed it home.

Behind him, the cabin groaned once and collapsed on itself with a heavy sigh resembling a man's final exhale, becoming a fifteen-foot heap of flickering rubble. Without the building's hungry flames leaping high into the air, visibility was abruptly and dramatically reduced.

Peering through the trees with his night-vision goggles, Bolan could see his adversary in a prone position behind his snowmobile, the stubby muzzle of his Uzi poking around the vehicle's front end. The man's partners had moved far enough away to be outside the halo emitted by the burning cabin, apparently playing the odds that their opponent would not be equipped with night vision. Considering what his course of action would be if the tables were turned, Bolan thought his enemies would take cover in one of the little snow gullies before attempting a flanking movement. He jumped onto his snowmobile, revved the powerful motor, and sped straight toward the gunman who had been attempting to pin him down while his partners maneuvered.

In an effort to reduce his profile as much as possible, Bolan hugged his snowmobile's fuselage as he shot out of the tree line on a direct course for the man lying in a covered position behind his vehicle. Making sure to maintain a straight-on approach to take advantage of the protection his snowmobile's windshield offered, Bolan fired the Desert Eagle with his left hand, holding the snowmobile's handlebars steady with his right.

The move obviously surprised his opponent, who hesitated for a fatal second before engaging the fast-approaching warrior with his Uzi, filling the night air with the chilling sound of automatic chatter. The 9 mm lead sprayed wildly across the space separating Bolan from his enemy. Bullets ricocheted off his bulletproof windshield as he charged forward at full throttle, covering the distance between him and his foe in less than thirty seconds. In a move resembling that of a bull-fighter, the Executioner swung outward at the last instant in order to avoid a collision, his Desert Eagle roaring death in triple-time tempo. A few rounds sparked upon impact with the gunman's Uzi a nanosecond before a pair of .44 rounds whizzing through the air in heel-to-toe configuration found the man's face, exploding his head in a crimson blossom. Bolan pulled hard on the snowmobile's handlebars while depressing the brake, causing the machine to slide sideways next to the dead man's vehicle. Throwing himself to the ground, he rolled into a prone position taking advantage of both snowmobiles for cover.

From his new location, he looked out beyond the pile of smoldering rubble of the cabin. One of his two remaining opponents was crawling toward the microwave cannon, while his partner engaged Bolan with a steady stream of lead from the relative safety of a snow gully approximately fifty feet away. Bolan drew his Beretta and fired the silenced weapon with his right hand while simultaneously blazing away with the Desert Eagle in his left, halting the man's progress toward the cannon and driving him back into the same gully as his teammate. A series of angry curses told him he had hit, albeit not fatally, the gunner trying to reach the microwave weapon.

With his enemies now occupying positions where they could battle him with only their heads exposed above the lip of the gully, the situation was classic trench warfare. Two adversarial forces separated by a no-man's land one hundred yards wide, with the microwave cannon occupying a position equidistant from both sides. In this situation, the day would belong to the combatant who could flush the other from cover.

Bolan holstered his Beretta, changed out magazines in the Desert Eagle and, while sporadically firing well-aimed shots to prevent his foes from advancing, reached into one of the pouches on his web belt containing a length of thin cord resembling braided dental floss. The three-hundred-foot length of specialty twine was fine enough to fold entirely in the palm of his hand while possessing all the strength of mountaineering rope.

Remaining behind the fuselage of his late adversary's snowmobile, Bolan reached up and wrapped a section of the cord around the vehicle's throttle to provide a steady fuel supply. When he turned the ignition key, the engine sprang to life, purring in neutral while he twisted the handlebars to aim the snowmobile toward the gully holding his foes. With the rounds from his Desert Eagle keeping his opponents pinned, Bolan used his free hand to unhook two concussion grenades from his combat belt's webbing and set the fuses to their maximum thirty seconds. Throwing the shift into gear, he dropped the apple-shaped bombs into the snowmobile's two cup holders and released the vehicle.

The snowmobile moved on a perfectly straight course from Bolan to the gully, where it toppled into the depression, carrying its lethal load into the trench occupied by the two gunmen. When the grenades detonated with an eardrum-throbbing concussion, they ignited the vehicle's gas tank, spraying the fuel through the trench in a firestorm reminiscent of a Vietnam napalm attack. The ferocious explosion left no doubt regarding its effectiveness, but Bolan had his Desert Eagle loaded, cocked and held at the ready when he walked to the edge of the snow gully to investigate the damage. His former adversaries were charred beyond recognition, calling to mind the corpse he had discovered inside the cabin.

The Executioner walked slowly back to his snowmobile, started the engine and drove to the microwave weapon. With a remaining section of the cord, he was able to securely attach the sled to his vehicle before setting off toward the North Dakota border approximately seven hours distant. When he got close to the States, he'd come into range of a telephone tower enabling him to make an encrypted call to Barbara Price, Stony Man Farm's mission controller. She would take care of the necessary cleanup and the retrieval of remains to be delivered to the families of the Nautech engineers.

The hunting horn had been sounded. There were miles to go before the Executioner would find rest.

2

Ali Ansari Hasseim squinted against the water's glare as he gazed southwest from the outskirts of Bandar-e Abbas, a biblical town on Iran's Persian coast across the channel from Qeshm Island. Below him sat the narrow Strait of Hormuz, through which twenty percent of the world's oil supply passed. The busy waterway was bordered by Iran, Oman's Musandam Peninsula and the United Arab Emirates. Were it not for the region's constant political unrest, the Iranian shoreline's rugged beauty and perfect climate would have the potential to make the locale one of the world's top vacation destinations. As it was, however, there were no vacationers in the vicinity. Most of those who ventured along the scenic trails traversed by Hasseim and his ilk were heavily armed with the intent to kill.

For centuries, the coastal strip on which Hasseim and his four companions stood had been recognized as a strategic key to controlling the entire Persian Gulf. Blocking the landlocked waterway's sole egress at the point where it emptied into the Indian Ocean's Gulf of Oman was a tactic used at a time when the only power available for ships came from either the wind or human rowers. In contemporary times, closing the Strait of

Hormuz would create a logjam, snarling military and commercial traffic alike. In such a situation, American warships patrolling the Gulf would be sitting ducks.

Wind gusts hugging the shoreline whipped a combination of sea salt and desert dust into thin clouds that raced across the land break. Hasseim avoided breathing the gritty mixture by pulling a corner of his black checkered kaffiyeh over his nose and mouth, covering the jagged scar that ran from his left earlobe to the edge of his lower lip, tugging his mouth into a perpetual frown.

In the distance, silhouetted against the horizon out beyond the islands of Hormoz and Larak, Hasseim could see the USS *Dwight D. Eisenhower,* one of the United States Navy's nuclear aircraft carriers. At the sight of the occupying force, Hassein's heartbeat quickened in anger. Bitter bile found its way into his mouth, causing him to turn from his companions while he lifted the corner of his kaffiyeh and spit the rancid liquid onto the ground where it was immediately absorbed into the dust.

His network of spies kept Hasseim informed as to the location of the other CVN-class ship in the region, enabling him to redirect missile deployments when necessary. The militia commander was fully aware that when the time arrived to punish the infidels for invading and occupying sacred soil, the window of opportunity would be short-lived. For a missile attack on multiple targets to be successfully coordinated, prior placement of troops and equipment was absolutely critical.

As he waited for his captives to be delivered, Hasseim mentally inventoried his militia's missile stocks. In the area around Bandar-e Lengeh at the mouth of the strait, trusted fighters possessed more than four hundred American-made FIM-92A Stinger missiles. The shoulder-launched weapons had been among tens of thousands provided by the CIA in 1979 to mujahideen guerrillas engaged in their nine-year war against the Soviets in Afghanistan. Two decades later, when Western forces responding to the 9/11 attacks toppled the country's Taliban government, they attempted to round up and confiscate an estimated thirty thousand residual Stingers. But in a swiftly deteriorating country where there were more pressing priorities for the NATO troops than disarming regional warlords, a hastily conducted campaign yielded less than six thousand missiles. The remainder were quickly reallocated throughout the Middle East to Islamic militias such as Hasseim's. With the ability to deliver a 2.2-pound high-explosive warhead at supersonic Mach 2 speed from a range of up to five miles, the thirty-five-pound highly portable Stingers were major assets for any militant organization.

In addition to the Stingers, Hasseim also had access to six hundred Soviet SA-7 Grail missiles that had been sold indiscriminately to anyone willing to meet the asking price when the Communist empire collapsed. Although Grails were considerably less accurate than the heat-seeking Stingers, they possessed a range of almost four miles and, in quantity, could overcome their accuracy deficiency and contribute significantly to overall success.

All told, Hasseim held the means to attack the two United States aircraft carriers patrolling the channel's narrow passageway at Hormuz with more than one thousand missiles. Troops to the southeast in Sirik would join fighters positioned in Bandar-e Lengeh at the mouth of the strait and across the waterway in Al Khasab to completely surround backlogged targets. Hundreds of missiles guided by infrared seekers would come raining down from all sides onto the enemy's warships, delivering a stunning statement about the technological capabilities possessed by local Islamic militias. While certainly not on par with the glorious 9/11 attacks conducted on the barbarians' own soil, Hasseim believed his offensive could be a decisive blow toward ending American occupation of the region. The only hurdle remaining was a computer system onboard American carriers that automatically shielded the vessels while engaging incoming targets. Hasseim now possessed one-half of a program that could disarm the protective system. If all went according to plan, he'd have the other half very soon.

At the moment, his activities were intended to misdirect the Americans. Hasseim didn't know if his plans would be discovered prior to launching an attack, but if they were, he wanted to make sure the Americans were searching in the wrong direction until he had the time he needed.

The four men accompanying their field commander were dressed in dark pants and brown shirts with long sleeves. On their feet they wore canvas combat boots, and each carried P-90 submachine guns.

The men also wore black checkered head scarves, identical to the kaffiyeh worn by their leader. Hasseim's army was one hundred percent Shiite, and in addition to their primary objective of driving the occupying infidels from their holy land, each member had also taken a solemn oath to eradicate the Sunni population responsible for polluting Islam.

A sudden movement in the distance caught Hasseim's eye. A battered white panel truck was speeding their way, trailing in its wake a yellow dust cloud reaching ten feet into the air. Hasseim nodded to his companions, who walked away from their SUV in order to put a buffer of safe distance between themselves. As they moved, they brought their P-90s to the ready position.

The truck bounced over the dusty coastal trail at breakneck speed, coming to a skidding halt ten feet from where Hasseim stood. The front doors flew open, and two men jumped out and hustled to the commander.

"Allah be praised," the first said breathlessly, "your servants have been blessed with success."

"You have them all?" Hasseim asked in a flat voice.

"Yes," the driver replied as he and his companion began moving toward the back of the truck. Hasseim followed a few steps behind, his P-90 loaded and cocked. His right index finger itched with anticipation as it rested on the weapon's trigger.

When they reached the vehicle's rear, the driver unlocked the back door and threw it open. On the floor inside, five men lay with their feet tied and their hands bound behind their backs with heavy nylon wrist wraps. Burlap bags covered their heads, loosely cinched at the throat with black shoelaces. Three were wearing United States Army uniforms, the unit patch on their left shoulders bearing the numeral one embroidered in red thread. They were members of The Big Red One—the Army's First Infantry Division.

Hasseim's lips curled into a cruel smile when he saw his quarry.

"The others?" he asked, indicating the two in civilian dress with the barrel of his P-90 submachine gun.

"Munjian," the driver responded, referring to a secondary Sunni militia operating along the Iraqi border.

Hasseim signaled to the men who had come with him, and they trotted to his side. He motioned toward the captives with his chin, and two bent into the truck, grabbed a soldier by the uniform and dragged him to the floor's edge. Upon being moved, the trussed man began jerking against his restraints, repeatedly arching his back until Hasseim took a step forward and gave the burlap bag covering the man's head a sharp rap with the butt of his submachine gun. The soldier stiffened at the blow and stopped squirming.

Once the bound prisoner was still, one of Hasseim's men gripped him under the armpits while another grabbed him around his knees. Grunting under the effort, they lifted the trussed American and hefted him clear of the truck's cargo hold, making space for their two teammates to duplicate their action with a second soldier. The truck's driver and his companion followed suit when the second team moved away, pulling the final soldier from the back of the truck. Staggering slightly, they followed the others, carrying their soldier from the vehicle toward a spot designated by Hasseim roughly twenty yards away. There the soldiers were thrown onto the ground to await their fate. Although they remained motionless, their raspy breathing could be heard through the burlap sacks covering their heads, as rapid and shallow as a trapped rabbit's.

"Move them apart," Hasseim ordered as he slung his P-90 over his shoulder. While his men obeyed his order, he walked to the panel truck's open passenger door, reached into the leg space in front of the seat and came out holding an Uru Model II submachine gun. The stockless 9 mm Brazilian assault rifle had a well-earned reputation for fouling when exposed to the slightest amount of moisture or dust in the chamber. Despite its notorious unreliability, the inexpensive weapon with its 30-round magazines was a favorite among Third World militias. The Sunni Munjian was known to have outfitted their members with Urus.

Hasseim rammed the rifle's slide to the rear and let it fly forward, chambering the first of the thirty slugs waiting inside the clip. After scanning the area with dispassionate eyes to make sure his men were clear, he pulled the weapon into his shoulder and, leaning forward slightly, opened fire on the trussed soldiers laying on the ground.

The Uru spit death on full-auto, filling the air with mind-panicking chatter. Hasseim swept the gun from left to right and back again, hosing the men from head to toe with lethal lead. The 9 mm slugs tore the corpses to pieces, slamming through flesh and bone before exiting through gaping holes the size of tennis balls. The Uru's firing pin finally clicked onto an open chamber, and the weapon fell silent.

Hasseim's eyes were glassy, his face flushed. He placed the Uru on the ground at his feet and turned to the truck's passenger seat. This time, he brought an American M-16 from the front leg well.

The two Sunni militiamen were chanting death prayers when they were pulled from the back of the truck to a spot thirty yards from the soldiers' corpses. There they were unceremoniously dumped onto the ground, and Hasseim reenacted his prior murderous action, spraying the captives with M-16 rounds.

When the magazine was exhausted, he lowered the rifle, his ears ringing from the auditory assault of the M-16's automatic barrage. His rapid breathing irritated the inside of his nostrils with the stench of death and cordite that now hung heavy in the late afternoon humidity. As his men rushed forward to cut the bonds from the dead men, he took a few steps back, handing the empty M-16 to one of his assistants. When Hasseim's men finished arranging the bodies, it would appear all had died in a firefight. Skirmishes between independent militia and NATO forces were an everyday occurrence in this region; there would be no reason for anyone to doubt the evidence.

"Abbas," Hasseim called out, bringing a thin young man with alert brown eyes to his side. "Give this to one of them," he said softly, holding out an eight-gigabyte memory stick wrapped tightly in a plastic sandwich bag.

Abbas took the memory stick and hustled to the side of the Sunni on the left as Hasseim began walking to his SUV. Only he and his driver would take the trip back, the others would remain to arrange the scene.

"The Americans will be alerted?" Hasseim asked the driver, although his tone conveyed the question was more a statement than an inquiry.

"Within hours. We'll give them GPS coordinates. They'll be here tonight," the driver replied.

Hasseim took a final look toward the water when they reached their vehicle. The sun was low, reflecting off the Gulf's rippled surface. In his mind, he pictured the narrow channel jammed with American warships. From the highlands above the strait, militiamen equipped with hundreds of missiles would find the unprotected vessels easy targets. Allah be willing, the remainder of the code would be delivered to his servants and the infidels would be destroyed.

Running a dry tongue over his chapped lips, Hasseim climbed into his SUV. For the first time since morning, he thought of his most recent partners in Las Vegas, the city that in Hasseim's mind, said all there was to say about Western civilization.

3

Stony Man Farm, Virginia

Hal Brognola was sitting at the conference table, engaged in quiet conversation with Carmen Delahunt and Akira Tokaido, two-thirds of what Aaron Kurtzman considered to be the best cybernetics team anywhere. They stopped talking and looked up when Mack Bolan stepped into the room.

"Striker," Hal Brognola greeted the warrior.

Bolan pulled a chair away from the conference table and slid in next to Delahunt.

"Something I didn't ask," he said, looking at Brognola as if they were in the middle of a conversation, "was how they came to our attention in the first place."

"Homeland Security phone monitoring," Brognola replied. "Key words and patterns flagged them for follow-up investigation. Akira started looking into their actions three weeks ago."

The hacker snapped his bubble gum a few times in rapid succession before saying, "Rookies. Lame attempts to cover their tracks. E-mail, phone and bank records are all over the place. They're definitely selling a code they say will disable ADAS."

From his seat a good six feet away, Bolan could hear a tinny percussive sound coming from Tokaido's high-fidelity earbuds. As he often did, he wondered how the young man could hear and carry on normal conversations while rock music was coursing at ear-splitting volume into his auditory canals.

"If we know who they are and what they're trying to do, why don't we just go get them?" Bolan asked.

The others looked directly at Brognola, who said, "Let's wait until everyone gets here. Carmen has to be brought up to date, too."

The wait was not long. Bolan poured himself a cup of coffee from the insulated carafe placed next to the cups. The coffee was a high-quality blend, not Kurtzman's horrid brew. He had barely taken his first sip when the door to the War Room opened.

Barbara Price entered first, followed by Huntington Wethers, then Kurtzman pushing his wheelchair forward with both hands, a cup of his infamously strong coffee in a holder mounted to the chair's left arm.

The three found places at the conference table, Price sitting directly across from Bolan, whom she greeted with a slight smile as she eased herself onto the upholstered cushion and pulled her seat closer to the table. Kurtzman moved to the open spot at the head as nonchalantly as if a chair had never occupied the space there.

"Who's up?" he asked while taking his brimming coffee cup from its holder and tasting a small mouthful of the steaming drink before putting it onto the conference table's highly polished surface.

"Let's get a summary," Brognola answered. "Striker asked how we initially latched on to them, and Carmen has been out of the loop. Akira?"

"Robbie Maxwell's group," Tokaido said, referring

to the team's contact at Homeland Security, "picked up keywords and phrases. Not sure if it was random. Home Security monitors employees at companies like Nautech more than ordinary citizens. After the initial alert, Maxwell put one of his guys into Nautech's facility in San Diego while we investigated four engineers whose names he gave us. Like I just said to Striker, they tried covering their tracks, but it was easy to trace phone calls and money deposits into numbered accounts in the Caymans. Each account received a deposit of five million dollars.

"Bank records led us to the four engineers," Tokaido continued, ticking off each name with his fingers. "Sherry Krautzer, David Thompson, Wesley Maple and Marlene Piaseczna. Maxwell's group was all set to arrest them when the four suddenly vanished."

"Security leak?" Wethers asked, displaying the methodological approach that Kurtzman had known would be a perfect complement to Delahunt's intuition skills.

"We thought so at first," Brognola jumped in to answer the question. "But Maxwell's guy was very discreet. These four were not tipped-off. They were just lucky."

"Not too lucky," Bolan said in a flat voice, remembering the names spoken by the young woman at the cabin who had identified herself as Sherry Krautzer. "Three of them are dead. Marlene Piaseczna is the only one who wasn't in Manitoba."

"We believe she's the ringleader," Brognola replied, "but Maxwell also thought there could be a fifth conspirator. Akira's money trail gives support to that idea. Twenty-one million withdrawn from the source banks, but only twenty million redeposited into the four accounts in the Caymans."

"I can see young engineers going on a wild spending spree," Delahunt said. "Fast cars, electronic gadgets, designer clothes and jewelry—a kid with money for the first time could go through a quarter mil in nothing flat."

"But they didn't," Brognola said. "We've been into their apartments. There's some evidence they were planning to leave the country, but they didn't go out and buy a bunch of stuff. That missing million bothers me."

"Did the Piaseczna woman betray her comrades?" Price asked.

"I don't think so," Bolan answered. "If there were separate accounts in the Caymans for each name individually—" he glanced at Tokaido, who gave him a confirming nod "—she wouldn't be able to get at her co-conspirators' money, so greed wasn't a motive. The killers in Manitoba tried to strong-arm the remaining code from the engineers there. They didn't have it. Piaseczna must be holding the second half the buyers wanted, and she was savvy enough to make sure everything would never be in one location."

"Striker's right," Brognola said. "Homeland Security couldn't put names to the killers' corpses you left at the cabin in Manitoba, but they're sure they were from the Middle East."

"Amateurs!" Kurtzman exploded from the end of the table. "Stupid engineers! Thinking they could hold back half the code and leverage it into providing protection for themselves. Didn't they realize their customers were cold-blooded murderers?"

"Never mind their customers," Brognola said. "What about their new partners?"

Turning to Bolan, he added, "You'll love this. Maxwell put some of his people on the money trail. It also leads to the McCarthy Family in Las Vegas.

"It seems," the man from Justice continued, "that our engineers hired McCarthy to be a go-between for the final piece. According to Maxwell's Las Vegas source, the remaining segment of code is apparently planned for delivery to one of McCarthy's men. McCarthy is passing it on to the terrorists, whoever they are."

"Slick move," Price said. "The engineers must have been terrified of their buyers. They thought delivering half the code would keep them safe until they got all their money. But they knew once their customers had the complete product there would be no reason not to kill them. So they hired the Mob to make the final delivery. Slick but stupid. Out of the frying pan. How reliable are Maxwell's sources, Hal?"

"They're good. After 9/11, Homeland Security realized the crime families might be tempted at some point to link up with a terrorist element. They have some deep plants in McCarthy's organization."

"How would young engineers in San Diego go about hiring the Mob? How would they get the initial contact?" Price asked.

"Too many possibilities," Wethers answered. "A friend of a friend's friend, an in-law connection, it could be anything. Pursuing that question is probably not worthwhile. More than that, I'd want to know how they linked up with the terrorists."

"Internet," Brognola said confidently. "Employees at defense firms, especially young engineers, are prime targets for subversive groups. If these engineers went looking, they'd easily find a buyer."

"But we don't know who that buyer is," Wethers interjected.

Brognola finger-combed his hair while shaking his head. "No, we don't."

Delahunt said, "It doesn't matter. The important fact is that someone has to get to McCarthy, find out where Piaseczna is planning to make the final drop-off and stop her from doing it."

"I agree," Price said. Looking across the table at Bolan. "I guess you're going to Sin City."

"What about the microwave weapon?" Kurtzman asked of the contraption now stored in one of the outbuildings on the compound.

"Marketing," Tokaido answered. "It's years behind microwave research, not state-of-the-art at all. I think they built it at their cabin to show they were real engineers. When Piaseczna contacted potential buyers, what did she have for credentials? Something like that gives a rogue engineer credibility."

"Then it served its purpose," Bolan stated. "And it led us to where we are."

He stared into the distance as if he could see through the walls to where the woman named Marlene Piaseczna was hiding.

"Rogue engineer, indeed," Kurtzman said softly. "Stop the sale, Striker. You have to make sure—" He was interrupted by the buzzing of his PDA, which he pulled from a pouch on the side of his wheelchair.

His face transformed into a frown as he held the module at arm's length and read the display.

"There was a firefight early this morning across the Iraqi border in Iran," he told the Stony Man Farm team. "A few United States soldiers and two Sunni were killed. One of them was carrying a piece of ADAS code."

"I think," Wethers said into the sudden silence, "we may have stumbled upon the buyers."

4

Bolan pushed through the bodies pressing against him on all sides. The sound of helicopter blades cut the night air, appearing to be coming from every direction. The mere sound of choppers swooping down from a black sky like prehistoric birds of prey was often enough to bring the fainthearted to the very brink of panic. As Bolan moved forward, the airships' ear-thumping reverberations stirred vestiges indelibly ingrained in his combat psyche, sending a rush of adrenaline to his brain. His eyes darted back and forth, constantly assessing and reassessing his environment as he made his way forward.

A silver beam shot to earth from one of the choppers, sweeping across the ground below as if searching for an escapee, pausing from time to time to randomly illuminate individuals who were pushed and pulled at the whim of the pulsating crowd. Off to Bolan's left, a series of underwater explosions sent steaming geysers swirling two hundred feet into the sky. Seconds later, the acrid smell of burning cordite reached his nostrils as yellow flames burst from the windows of concrete buildings erected behind the dock where a fully rigged pirate ship bobbed on the moat's gentle ripples. The leaping flames illuminated the stage in a flickering light.

The Sirens of TI battle, enacted four times nightly in the wide moat adjacent to Treasure Island's Las Vegas hotel, was one of the Strip's most popular free attractions. People stood five and six deep on the walkways surrounding the waterway, jockeying for space a good fifteen minutes before the mock battle's first cannon was scheduled to be fired. Above, tourists of greater affluence viewed the performance from chartered helicopters.

The flaming dock and exploding depth charges were part of the show's final sequence, which meant the sidewalk traffic was about to go from bad to worse. Kept perfectly on cue by computerized commands, a gaudy fireworks volley blossomed into intricate designs against the black sky, reflecting in the windows of the ultramodern Wynn Hotel across the Strip. The building's curving architecture acted like a concave mirror, adding an extra dimension of depth to the pyrotechnics display.

Bolan increased his pace while mentally reviewing everything he knew about Michael McCarthy.

The gangster was third-generation Vegas, his Family having been one of the first to move in with serious muscle back when the Strip was little more than a gas stop for GIs on their way to San Diego and Tijuana from Army and Air Force posts in the heartland. The current McCarthys were still involved in their Family's original businesses—guns, prostitution and drugs. Bolan's previous encounters with the clan had been personal in nature, resulting in one entire branch of the family tree undergoing a rather severe pruning.

Michael McCarthy ran his drug business out of an auto body repair shop up on Freemont and South Seventeenth, servicing the entire Strip to the south, and north a good ten miles beyond downtown. According to Brognola, the man had a hair-trigger temper and a reputation for lashing out at whoever happened to be within slapping range. In the past decade he had thrice been indicted on murder charges, all of which vanished as completely as the key witnesses.

Bolan was dressed in dark chinos and a cotton jersey underneath a navy-blue Windbreaker. An extra swatch of cloth had been expertly sewn into the jacket's left breast, concealing the telltale bulge where his Beretta 93-R sat in its soft leather holster. The semiautomatic pistol, with its stubby sound suppressor extending the barrel an additional two inches, was primed for action. A 20-round clip of 9 mm steel-jacketed Parabellum rounds occupied the ammo port, a twenty-first slug already chambered.

On his feet, the combat veteran wore cross-training shoes reinforced with a small steel plate in the toe.

McCarthy's shop sat back from the street in a section of Vegas not often frequented by tourists. As in many cities, the demarcation line separating safety from danger in Las Vegas was a fuzzy one. Despite sales pitches hawked by travel agents pushing package deals for hotel accommodations "just off the Strip," the unwary tourist visiting Las Vegas could easily stumble into the type of neighborhood he or she would never enter at home. Although Bolan's destination was less than a ten-minute walk from the Strip's northern edge, it existed in a world far removed from the one portrayed in glitzy sales brochures.

McCarthy's business occupied an entire block in a section that bridged the gap between visitor friendly and dangerously derelict. The location was perfect for the crime boss. The front office housed drug runners who worked out of cubicles taking orders and delivering the product throughout McCarthy's territory. The backyard bordered an area where the seedier elements of society could be accessed as required.

Without altering his pace, Bolan walked by on lower Freemont Street, keeping his eyes to the front while he reconnoitered the building using his peripheral vision. To a casual passerby, he was a man completing an errand—moving purposely but not hurriedly, confident of where he was going and what needed to get done. A more intuitive observer might pick up a somewhat disconcerting vibe that he was a man of danger, and any attempt to thwart his efforts might not bode well.

McCarthy's actual repair shop, where legitimate automotive work was done by certified mechanics, was a two-story concrete structure attached to the east side of the brick office building. Two men leaning against one of the triple bay garage doors smoked cigarettes in silence, their eyes tracking Bolan's progress as he passed. The door for the middle bay was open, spilling bare-bulb light into the night. From within, a symphony of power grinding and metal-on-metal pounding sang out.

Bolan turned up the walkway to the office building's front door. Out of the corner of his eye, he could see the two smokers pushing themselves away from their spot and angling toward him, their cocky swagger telling him they were no strangers to trouble.

"What do you want?" one man asked when they came close. The speaker was short and swarthy, with a thick black mustache hugging the top of a thin set of lips. As he waited for a response, he used his tongue to shift a toothpick from one corner of his mouth to the other.

The pair stopped when they were in tight, less than three feet. The one who had been silent thus far said, "Answer the man, dude." His breath stank of garlic and beer.

"I'm here to see McCarthy," Bolan stated.

"He didn't say no one was coming."

The man stood a little over six feet and possessed an alertness that suggested he may have once been an athlete. The soft paunch spilling over his belt buckle in untidy ripples indicated he had embraced a lifestyle of habits somewhat different from what his routine had probably been during his playing years. He tilted his head slightly and pointed his chin at Bolan, exposing a bulging Adam's apple protruding from the middle of long skinny neck.

"Tell him there's a man from Washington who would like a few minutes of his time. He doesn't know my name."

"Maybe you don't understand. He didn't say no one was coming."

Keeping his eyes on the pair, Bolan reached out to ring the doorbell.

An instant before the taller man moved, Bolan anticipated his action. The Executioner instinctively jerked his head to one side as the man's fist jabbed the air, passing a hairbreadth from his face. With the breeze from the missed blow caressing his cheek, Bolan took a quick step forward, driving a handful of stiff fingers into his attacker's throat. The man coughed and clutched at his neck with both hands, stumbling back a few feet. His legs buckled and he fell to one knee, fighting to suck in air.

Before his victim's partner could react, Bolan unleashed a rapid flurry of short punches to his face. The blows dislodged the toothpick from its perch, sending it flying through space on a wave of saliva. The man attempted to strike back, but he was falling away from Bolan's volley, his momentum pulling him in the wrong direction. His return jabs landed harmlessly on his adversary's muscular forearms.

The warrior stepped back to place a little distance

between them. The taller man continued to gasp and wheeze while holding his throat with both hands. He attempted to rise, but when he was halfway upright, appeared to lose his balance and went back to one shaky knee. His bulging eyes indicated he was having serious trouble getting oxygen to his lungs.

Turning his attention to the man still standing, Bolan jabbed twice more with the precision of a prizefighter, efficiently opening a cut above his opponent's left eye before making direct impact with the bridge of his nose, breaking the cartilage. His victim staggered back a few steps, breathing raggedly. As he spit a thick glob of bloody phlegm toward Bolan, he reached into his pants pocket and pulled out a switchblade. He didn't know it, but he was about to learn a lesson in arms proliferation—escalation always led to greater violence. His punishment would be more severe than that dealt to his partner.

The man's eyes were gleaming with unbridled hatred as he pressed the release and a three-inch blade snapped into place. A beam of errant light spilling out from the bulb above the office building's door caught the knife's edge, making it shine an instant before Bolan crouched and launched himself into a counterclockwise spin, his right foot tracing a roundhouse arc through the air. The steel toe of his shoe made direct contact with the man's wrist, shattering the delicate bones. The switchblade flew into the distance, clattering onto the sidewalk as Bolan completed his move. Using his momentum, he allowed his motion to flow smoothly into a second kick aimed at his opponent's chin. His toe struck dead center, violently jerking the man's head up and back. The man went down to the walkway like a ton of bricks, where he lay unconscious.

From the corner of his eye, Bolan saw a man emerge

from the repair shop's center bay at the same time he heard the distinctive sound of a sawed-off shotgun being cocked. He took a quick step away from his adversaries and raised his hands over his head.

"Yeah, you'd better keep 'em up," the gunman said, swiftly closing the distance between them. "Who are you, and what do you want?"

"I'm here to see McCarthy," Bolan said.

"Is he expecting you?"

"No. I'm here from Washington. He'll want to hear what I came to say."

From his position on one knee, the taller man hitched and wheezed as he fought to breathe. His partner groaned and moved his fingers slightly before relapsing into total unconsciousness.

"Help T.J. get up," the shotgun carrier said to the taller man. "Go on, get him out of here. I'll bring this guy in to see the boss."

The tall man nodded and staggered to his feet, glaring at Bolan.

"Get Billy to help you with him," the gunman said.

The injured thug ambled unsteadily away on legs as unsure as those of a newborn foal.

The man with the shotgun said, "You can put your hands down, but I'll fill your hide with buckshot the second you make a false move."

Bolan dropped his hands.

From inside the office building, a woman started screaming the way people do when they're receiving a beating. The voice behind the shotgun said, "It's unlocked."

Bolan opened the door onto a high-ceilinged bull pen populated from front to back with chest-high cubicles, each space containing a chair and desk with phone. A few dozen men worked the lines, talking softly into the mouthpieces, oblivious to the woman's shrieks, which appeared to be coming from a closed office at the far end of the bull pen. Had the scene been filmed and shown on mute, the crime syndicate's fronting operation could have been mistaken for a Wall Street trading office.

"All the way to the back," the man with the shotgun said.

Bolan walked through the cubicles to the office, barely raising an eyebrow from anyone as he passed. Outside the closed door, a massive man dressed in a black suit with matching black shirt and tie stood. With arms crossed, he watched Bolan's approach through half-closed eyelids. The man was Johnny Kohotina, a Hawaiian ex-con who had served as Michael McCarthy's personal bodyguard for more than a decade. Bolan recognized the six-foot-six mountain of sculptured muscle from pictures Hal Brognola had shown him back at Stony Man Farm.

Kohotina made a questioning motion with his head. The woman's cries had subsided, but from up close Bolan could hear blows striking flesh. The victim inside the office may have been losing consciousness, but the beating continued.

"He says he's from Washington," the man behind Bolan said in response to Kohotina's implied question. "The boss don't like Feds nosing around without knowing what they want."

Kohotina pursed his full lips into a rosebud and stared into the distance. "Yeah," he replied, saying the word as if it contained two syllables.

The office door suddenly opened and two men emerged. One was carrying an unconscious woman hefted over his shoulder in a fireman's hold. She was wearing a long dress made of expensive-looking silk. The ease with which the man held her slender body indicated she was a lightweight, an impression her skinny arms reinforced when they walked past Bolan. As the trio went by, Bolan could hear soft moans coming from the woman. She was bleeding from her head and face, leaving a trail of droplets on the floor and down the back of her transporter's shirt.

"Go ahead," the man with the shotgun said. Kohotina stared hard at them as they entered the office.

Michael McCarthy was sitting behind his desk, wiping fresh blood from his knuckles with a terry-cloth hand towel. His face was flushed, beads of perspiration stood out on his forehead and he was breathing shallowly. He paused for a moment and caressed his cheek with the back of his hand, almost as if he was forgetting what he was doing. When he glanced up, Bolan saw that the whites of his eyes were filled with a tangle of bloodshot squiggles.

He sniffed a few times, asked, "What the fuck do you want?"

"The Feds know all about your drug operation," Bolan said. "Suppliers, routes, distributors. They also know about the illegals you're working as whores."

"Koko! Get in here," McCarthy shouted.

As they waited, Bolan noticed a small table in the corner of the room on which a mirror, a few razor blades and two short metal tubes sat. McCarthy's bloodshot eyes and mannerisms took on new significance. It wasn't rare for a violent man to become even more so while using cocaine.

The bodyguard came into the room, pulling the door closed behind him.

"This a shakedown?" McCarthy asked in quick time.

"No. A business proposition," Bolan said.

"You carrying?"

"I am."

McCarthy made a come hither motion with the fingers of one hand, said, "Let's have it."

Bolan reached into his Windbreaker, drew his Beretta 93-R and placed it on the edge of the desk where it was within grasping range if the need arose. In his mind, he saw himself dive next to the desk, snatching the pistol in midflight. Before he hit the floor, he'd twist and kill the man with the shotgun. The bodyguard would be next.

"Here's the deal," Bolan said in a calm voice.

McCarthy was staring at his visitor as if he had two heads. It wasn't often that a man walked right into his office, told him about his crime operation, admitted to being armed, then put his piece on the desk in plain view.

"You have a cozy relationship right now with the Feds," Bolan continued. "They don't bother you too much, and they've realized they can't completely stop what you do. So you both kind of keep each other in line. What happens in Vegas, right? But now there's something else."

He looked straight at McCarthy. "The Navy computer code. We don't know when or where you're picking it up from Marlene Piaseczna. But that's what we want. We'll go get it instead of you."

Bolan had more know-how about the areas of interrogating and being interrogated than most people on the planet. Throughout his career he had personally used every technique known, and had also been the victim of both legal and illegal interrogations. One thing he had gained from his extensive experience on both sides of the table was an uncanny sense of knowing when a man was telling the truth. Sometimes, the subject didn't even have to speak.

Such was the case now. Based on McCarthy's subtle reaction, and a fleeting moment when something intangible passed behind his eyes, Bolan knew without a doubt that Maxwell's intel was good.

"Don't know what you're saying," the crime boss replied. He sniffed a few times, glanced over his shoulder at the table in the corner, then returned his gaze to Bolan. "And if I did, why would I turn? What are you offering?"

"A chance for you to avoid some serious pain."

"Get him out of here," McCarthy said as his face quickly took on the hue of a ripe tomato.

He slapped the surface of his desk with both hands. "You think you can come in here and run me?" he shouted. "I oughta send you back in pieces! The only thing saving your ass is that I don't know who you are. But you'd better tell whoever sent you that no one tells Michael McCarthy what deals he can make! No one!"

In a motion belying his size, Kohotina's hand moved in a blur, reaching into his suit coat and emerging with a .40-caliber Glock. The semiautomatic handgun pointed at Bolan appeared ridiculously small in the bodyguard's grasp.

"Okay," Bolan said, holding his hands palms up. "My people will not be happy."

"Fuck your people! Get out of here before I decide to kill you," McCarthy shouted.

Bolan reached for his Beretta.

"Uh-uh," McCarthy said, shaking his head back and forth in an exaggerated motion. "I'm taking that home with me. Disrespect to whoever sent you. Now get the hell out before I take your balls, too."

Staring at McCarthy, Bolan calculated the time it would take to snatch his Beretta, drill a hole into the forehead of the Hawaiian, then turn and plug the man standing behind him holding the sawed-off shotgun. The question was one of reflexes. If the tables had been turned and he was the one holding the Glock, he knew that a prisoner in his position would be killed the instant he leaned toward the desk.

Combat veterans with backgrounds similar to Bolan's fully understood the difference between bravery and stupidity. Without another word, Bolan turned on his heel and walked to the office door.

Once outside on the sidewalk, he pulled his cell phone from his pants pocket and speed dialed one of Brognola's secure lines.

Bolan didn't think Andrew B. Tommison IV would have a Beretta 93-R readily available in stock, but he firmly believed the Las Vegas arms dealer would have a substitute weapon he could use for a day or so until McCarthy handed his pistol back to him.

5

Four hundred miles west of her home port of San Diego, aircraft carrier CVN-76, christened USS *Ronald Reagan,* was undergoing sea trials prior to her deployment to the Persian Gulf. Being nuclear powered, the U.S. Navy's newest carrier could operate for more than twenty years without refueling, but running out of gas wasn't even a blip on Petty Officer Timothy Bergeron's radar screen. Assigned to the Combat Systems Department, subgroup CS-7, Bergeron's mission during the trials was to ensure all electronic interfaces connecting ADAS to peripheral radar and weapons systems were fully operational. Bergeron's computer skills were considerable, but the complexity of the sea trials, designed to simulate worst-case scenarios, would push his concentration to the very limits of his talent. Not unlike a long-distance runner fidgeting with his shoelaces and socks at the starting line prior to the race, Bergeron adjusted the angle of his computer monitor and checked for the fifth or sixth time that the water bottle in the holder mounted to his chair was full.

The communications petty officer took his Navy responsibilities very seriously, going so far as to have visited Nautech Corporation's facility in San Diego on his own time while he was out on shore leave. At

Nautech, with his young wife of less than a year sitting in a rented car in the company's parking lot, Bergeron had spent half a day talking with engineers who designed the system that now protected his life and the lives of his five thousand shipmates. While there, he had also met with a team of software engineers who wrote the operational code that ran ADAS. One of those engineers was now onboard, sitting next to Bergeron at the system's control console.

Assigned by the company as a ship rider to assist *Reagan*'s crew during one of the sea trial's particularly difficult segments, Leon Kreamer was no stranger to sea duty. Himself an ex-Navy computer whiz, Kreamer had been serving as one of two Nautech consultants on the USS *Eisenhower* when she sailed through the Straits of Magellan during a blizzard that rocked the carrier with hurricane-force winds creating waves hundreds of feet high. Back at Nautech, Kreamer had described the horrific voyage as the most awesome ride he had ever experienced. The other consultant with him, a software engineer named Marlene Piaseczna, had written in her trip report that the two-month assignment was one of the worst times of her life.

As part of the *Reagan*'s prove-out, software uplink capabilities would be tested, simulating a condition at sea when new versions of code would be installed. The technology for wireless uplink was new, utilizing line-of-sight data transmission via infrared courier beams, and no one in the Navy was skilled in its application. Kreamer, who was considered by Nautech's upper management to be one of their brightest engineers, would guide the command crew through the procedure.

Bergeron gazed across the bridge at Chief Warrant Officer Mike Herbert. In the crimson glow of the dim red lights used to illuminate the command center, it was hard to read what Herbert thought of the trials so far. Lighting on the *Reagan*'s bridge was designed to be soft on eyes that would stare for hours at radar screens and computer monitors.

Numerous Navy studies had shown that the subdued red lighting in a ship's command center dramatically reduced the eyestrain computer operators often experienced. But the overall effect was an eerie one. Each day when Bergeron reported for duty, he had the sensation he was entering a womb, a feeling further enhanced by a soft background pulsing from the sync clock that kept all systems in phase. Despite the weirdness, however, Bergeron liked everything—the lighting, the subdued sounds, the heightened sense of urgency—about the command center's environment. For him, it was a small sphere of serenity on a carrier where organized chaos was the norm.

Chief Herbert walked to a spot behind Bergeron and Kreamer where he could look over their shoulders at the ADAS display screen. The chief was *Reagan*'s weapons officer, responsible during trials to manage interfaces connecting the ship's weapons inventory to ADAS. During an attack, the Air Defense Alert System would detect and track all incoming objects within a thirty-nautical-mile radius, perform friend-or-foe analysis, select a weapon from available inventories based on the incoming's size and speed, and lock on to the threat. Before ADAS could actually engage a target with live fire, however, the weapons officer was required to activate the automatic-fire capability the system possessed. During sea trials, the automatic-fire capability was disabled, as the tests were intended to measure the crew's readiness as well as that of the hardware.

In the background, the sounding of ship's bells regis-tered in Bergeron's subconscious. Two chimes, pause, two chimes, indicating the morning watch was half over. In the civilian world, people would say it was six o'clock.

"Incoming," Bergeron said softly, his eyes tracking the simulated threat as soon as it appeared in the upper right corner of his screen.

In the middle of the monitor, the aircraft carrier sat like the center of a bull's-eye, surrounded by two concentric circles representing fifteen and thirty nautical miles.

"Eighteen degrees, Mach 2.5."

"Amram," Herbert replied, indicating his weapon choice.

Bergeron's fingers flew over the keyboard while Kreamer watched the action with a satisfied look on his face. He was proud of his company's product, and enjoyed seeing actual sailors work the system with as much skill and savvy as the electronic gamers he went head-to-head against in weekend tournaments spon-sored by leading software manufacturers.

A blip representing a supersonic Amram missile streaked out from the inner circle's center, speeding straight into the incoming target.

"Sweet," Kreamer said as both target and missile blinked off the screen.

Before Bergeron could respond, the screen was filled with attacking objects coming from every quadrant. Each item was tagged with a symbol representing speed and azimuth, a code both Bergeron and Herbert could read as easily as if the words were spelled out in large block letters.

"Sparrow. Sparrow. Tartar. Amram. Amram. CIWS," Herbert said in one breath. There was no need for him to specify which targets he was applying weapons to;

he and Bergeron had drilled for more than one hundred hours so they'd know without thinking what the order of engagement was.

With his hands moving back and forth in a blur between the console's trackball and keyboard, Bergeron fired missiles and deck guns, while Chief Herbert continued to call out weapons, his eyes darting from the ADAS screen to the automatic status boards mounted on brackets in the ceiling. The electronic boards kept track of missile inventories, allowing the weapons officer to manage his ship's firepower as he would if he were engaged in actual combat.

The simulated attack continued in waves for slightly more than five minutes, a period that to Bergeron seemed to last for hours. By the time the final incoming threat blinked off the screen, he was drenched in sweat, his throat parched. An alarm sounded, indicating the test segment was over. Bergeron reached for his water bottle and took a long swig, his Adam's apple bobbing up and down as he chugged the contents.

"Bravo Zulu, young man. Bravo Zulu!" Herbert said, complimenting his petty officer's performance with a hearty clap on the younger man's shoulder.

Before Bergeron had a chance to reply, a string of numbers flew across the screen from left to right, disappearing at the junction where glass met the border bezel. The speeding characters had been visible for less than two seconds.

"Did you see that?" he asked, pointing his water bottle at the screen.

"What?" Herbert responded.

"Yeah," Kreamer said. "Ping attack?"

Bergeron jammed the water bottle back into its holder and punched a few keys in rapid succession. "No."

"What?" Chief Herbert repeated.

"Looked like some kind of intrusion," Kreamer answered. "Six groups of eight?"

"More," Bergeron said. "Eight or twelve groups I think."

"Check the log," Kreamer said.

Bergeron leaned over the keyboard and typed a few sentences that caused his monitor to go blank for an instant before refreshing. The time clock in the screen's upper-left corner told him he was viewing a recording that had played real-time four minutes earlier. Kreamer pulled his chair close, his eyes glued to the screen as the clock ran down, approaching the present.

"Here it comes," the Nautech engineer said when the timer showed one minute remaining.

The three men watched as the clock ran out and the display resumed real-time tracking.

"It didn't record?" Kreamer asked. "How could it not?"

Bergeron turned in his chair and said, "You're asking me? You're the software engineer."

Chief Herbert asked, "What's the big deal? The system worked great, didn't it?"

"Yeah, it did," Kreamer said, staring over the console into the distance. His brow was furrowed, and his fingers had started tapping the side of Bergeron's work station.

"But the number string was an event that should not have been there. I don't like things like that. Something in the software just told the system something." He paused, ran his fingers through his hair and sat back in his chair. "Open an EDR," he said, referring to an engineering discrepancy report, the form utilized by Navy personnel to report electronic system failures.

"What's the fault?" Bergeron asked.

"Just say unknown characters. Say they appeared

after—" he reached out and grabbed the sea trial logbook that lay open on top of Bergeron's console, running his finger down a column of numbers "—after series 424 testing."

Bergeron nodded and scribbled a note to himself on the pad positioned to the left of the keyboard.

Kreamer gazed up at the ceiling, a puzzled expression on his face. "How could it not record?" he asked no one in particular.

ANDREW B. TOMMASIN IV had met the man before under similar circumstances. He hadn't enjoyed the encounters. It wasn't that the arms dealer felt physically threatened by his visitor's presence, nor did he fear his customer was an undercover state or local cop. The man's appearance had once again been preceded by a telephone call from the United States Department of Justice requesting a favor, and a person couldn't get much more connected than that. But there was something unsettling about the way the man went from one display case to another, as if he were seeking a spiritual bond or something with the merchandise.

Just pick a goddamn piece, the arms broker wanted to shout, but truth be known, this dude was one scary hombre. Even for someone in Tommasin's business, it was frightening to watch the man touch each weapon with a studied expression on his face as if he was reviewing in great detail the capability each product possessed. For no reason he could put into words, Tommasin had the distinct impression his customer was recalling memories he could associate with each weapon.

"You don't have a 93-R?" Bolan asked.

"No," Tommasin replied, avoiding eye contact. "I

don't have any Berettas at all right now." He hesitated for a second before saying, "I can order one for you."

The words were spoken in a rush as the weapons dealer suddenly saw a way to bring their awkward meeting to an abrupt end. "It'll be here tomorrow."

Drilling him with eyes that looked as if they were lit from behind by a raging fire, Bolan replied, "I'll have my own back by then," in a voice that made the hairs on the back of Tommasin's neck bristle.

Silence hung heavy between them in the cramped display room concealed behind false walls in the basement of a pornography shop on Vegas Valley Drive. Upstairs, the lighting was a mixture of neon blue and orange, setting an appropriate ambiance for the product line. The basement illumination, however, was stark and bright, supplied by three overhead banks of incandescent bulbs. The customers who purchased product downstairs wanted to make sure they saw everything before buying. Down here, nothing was left to the imagination.

"I have," Tommasin's began, but his voice caught in a suddenly dry throat. He swallowed, ran his tongue over his lips and said, "I have a few Walthers."

"PPK?"

"Three. New."

"Let's see 'em," Bolan said.

Tommasin pointed to a display case at the room's far end. As they walked toward it, Bolan paused for a moment to pick up a Spectre SMG. Less than fourteen inches long with its stock folded, the Italian submachine gun fired 9 mm slugs at the mind-numbing rate of 850 rounds per minute from a cleverly designed box magazine capable of holding fifty cartridges.

"That's a great zip gun," Tommasin said, sensing he might be selling more than a pistol. "Ever use one?"

"Yeah," Bolan replied. He put the weapon back down. "Not today."

They reached a display case holding an odd assortment of new and used handguns. Tommasin motioned to the weapons and said, "Take your pick."

"Ammo?"

"Depends on your choice. For the Walthers and Browning, I have standard and ACP. I have hollowpoint for the Imbel."

"Do the PPKs have silencers?" Bolan asked, pointing to the three pistols at the rear of the display.

"I only have one. All three are threaded, though."

The Executioner reached forward and took one of the Walthers. With hands that obviously had performed the routine before, he racked the slide to the open position and ran his pinky along the inside of the chamber, reaching back to touch the hammer's firing pin, then forward to where the barrel intersected with the ammo port. Pulling the slide back slightly to release the stop, he let it close on an empty chamber.

"I'll take this one," Bolan said, "with the silencer." He paused for a moment before adding, "I want extra clips. Two dozen with ACP rounds."

"I have longer magazines," Tommasin said. "A dozen twelve-rounders, or eight holding eighteen will give you the same one-forty-four."

"I can do the math. I don't want a clip sticking out the bottom that much."

Tommasin nodded while opening a drawer built into the lower half of the display case where a number of small leather bags resembling shaving kits lay in a flat pile. He pulled one out, placed the pistol inside and reached to the back of the drawer where he found a sound suppressor wrapped in pink antistatic bubble wrap. He slid the metal tube into the bag alongside the PPK's barrel.

"ACP .380 cartridges," he said as he walked toward a four-drawer file cabinet in the corner close to the door. "Ninety-five grain FMJs."

"Yeah. You have the tape and grenades?" Bolan asked.

"As requested."

At the file cabinet Tommasin counted out twenty-four stubby PPK magazines long enough to hold six rounds while being short enough to fit inside the pistol's handgrip. After placing them in the leather bag, he handed his customer an unopened box containing 144 rounds.

"Incendiary tape," he said, pulling out the drawer below the one containing the ammunition and retrieving a sealed plastic bag and two tubes roughly the size of travel toothpaste. "And two MK3A2s."

He handed the apple-sized concussion grenades to his customer, who shoved them into the right pocket of his navy-blue Windbreaker on top of the tape and tubes of reagent.

Taking the leather bag from the weapons dealer, Bolan asked, "You're all set?"

"Right as rain," Tommasin answered, relieved to be concluding the transaction.

The Executioner gave him a curt nod, walked down the aisle to the end and slid open the disguised door to the basement. Once outside the secret room, which was obviously soundproofed, the heavy metal rock music that played nonstop in the porn shop above could be heard coming through the ceiling.

"This way," Tommasin said, indicating a back exit.

Without a word, the man walked ahead of Tommasin

up a short flight of stairs leading to a back alley in one of the city's seediest, most dangerous sections.

Watching the man disappear into the night, the thought occurred to Tommasin that he was hoping there were not any gang members or muggers around who occasionally preyed on people who found themselves alone in this area. The arms dealer's general concern was not for his customer's welfare.

6

Michael McCarthy spent his nights in the top-floor penthouse suite of an eighty-story hotel situated five miles as the crow flies from McCarran International Airport. He also owned floors seventy-five through seventy-nine which, except for the live-in guards, were kept vacant as a security buffer. The only elevator with access to McCarthy's floor required a special key, and the stairwells on the five floors immediately below were kept locked with combination tumblers. A dozen guards armed with automatic assault rifles were in residence around the clock, ensuring that any attack on McCarthy's penthouse by a rival Family attempting to expand their muscle into Las Vegas would be a costly endeavor.

After taking off from the airport, the private Learjet carrying Bolan flew to the north, quickly gaining altitude. It was the same aircraft that the day before had brought him from Virginia to Las Vegas, piloted by the same ex-Navy ace named Mitch Davidson. Three minutes into the flight, he executed a 180-degree turn and headed south over Sin City.

Through the open door a few feet aft of the jet's starboard wing, Bolan gazed down at Fremont Street. Davidson had flown a practice run earlier in the day when it was still light, and told him the drop zone came up fast. Once they passed over downtown they'd quickly reach the Strip's neon extravaganza, en route to the Luxor Hotel and Mandalay Bay at the Strip's south end. As soon as Bolan saw the Luxor's pyramids with their spectacular water fountains, he'd hop out the door and begin his free fall.

Because he was free-falling and pulling his own rip cord, exit technique was not an issue for Bolan as he eased himself from the small Learjet into the desert air over Las Vegas. Dressed entirely in black, with camouflage battle paint smeared on his face and hands to soften their profiles and reflective glare, the Executioner was little more than a shadow as he flew through the pitch-black night.

On his hip, he wore his trusty .44-caliber Desert Eagle, locked and loaded with a custom 12-round clip of steel-jacketed slugs. In the shoulder holster designed to hold his Beretta 93-R, he carried the Walther PPK he had purchased earlier that evening from Tommasin. With sound suppressor attached, the weapon was a bit smaller than his Beretta. As a result, there was some play in the pocket, but it wasn't an issue because Bolan didn't plan on keeping either of his handguns holstered for long. A razor-sharp foot-long Sykes-Fairbairn combat knife in a black leather sheath was strapped to the outside of his right calf. Pouches clipped to his combat belt contained the incendiary tape, concussion grenades and spare ammo he needed for the mission.

Strapped on his back, Bolan wore an Aerodyne Mamba 9 cell elliptical parachute, with a custom-designed smaller chute pack tucked against his chest above his combat belt. At fifteen hundred feet, he pulled the rip cord, and a soft pop reached his ears as the black silk canopy opened. Knowing that the dark parachute and his own dress would blend into the night sky, he had deployed purposely high to give himself time to reconnoiter the rooftop of McCarthy's hotel on the way down. It was a gentle glide, easily controlled by the chute's expertly designed controls.

Bolan could see two guards on duty on the rooftop of McCarthy's hotel. One was walking casually along the north side of the building, maintaining a buffer of a few feet from the waist-high parapet that ran around the entire perimeter of the roof as a safety measure to keep people from falling off. Directly opposite from him, his partner was leaning against the barrier, scanning the windows in the hotel across the street with a pair of binoculars.

McCarthy's hotel occupied a footprint roughly the area of a quarter block, making the surface of the roof approximately the size of four football fields. Heating and air-conditioning ducts, compression stations, electrical relay houses and water treatment tanks stood in random clusters in the middle of the roof space, putting the men out of sight of each other most of the time. Both were armed with Heckler & Koch MP-5 submachine guns, slung across their backs. From his position a hundred feet above, Bolan could see the assault rifles' profiles. Both were equipped with suppressors, the thick tubes extending the barrels an additional foot beyond their foregrips.

During the final moments of his descent, Bolan worked the chute controls so he'd approach the guard with binoculars from the front. He didn't want the man dropping the field glasses over the side of the parapet to the sidewalk below where they might draw attention to the rooftop at an inopportune moment. As he tugged the chute's cord to rotate into position, Bolan drew the Walther PPK with his right hand.

As he passed within sight of the guard peering through binoculars, the man fumbled for his weapon. Bolan squeezed the Walther's trigger once. The handgun whispered instant death, and a neat hole the size of a dime immediately appeared in the middle of the man's forehead. Still holding his binoculars, he toppled backward onto the rooftop's pebbly surface, the assault weapon slung across his back making a grating sound upon contact.

"Hey, Billy," the guard's partner shouted from the other side of the roof. "Billy, you hear something? You okay?"

"Yeah," Bolan shouted back. Coughing loudly, he added, "Wait a minute," speaking in a rush so his voice might not betray him.

Dropping to one knee close to the guard's body, Bolan hurriedly gathered in the parachute, grabbing the folds into a bunch at the same time he released the harness. The chute fell free, a pile of nylon and thin cord weighing no more than a pound. Bolan rolled the material into a ball, and to keep it from catching the wind and fluttering up, pushed it under the dead man's head as if it were a pillow. Once the chute was secured, he quickly crept into the dark shadow the parapet offered. With his back pressing against the parapet, his black clothing and camouflaged face enabled him to effectively disappear.

When Bolan heard the other guard coming toward him from behind a grouping of seven or eight air-conditioning units, he leveled the Walther PPK at the point where he thought the man would appear. The approaching footsteps suddenly stopped, and the scritch of a cigarette lighter reached Bolan's ears as the condemned man lit his final smoke. The sound of a heavy exhale followed by a quick cough preceded the resumption of steps, coming slowly but not in a manner indicating caution.

Bolan's wait was not long. The guard came around the corner, smoking his cigarette and walking with a gait more suitable for a stroll in the park than for sentry duty. He stopped short as soon as he caught sight of his partner's prone body, doing a double take that in other circumstances might have been comical.

He dropped his cigarette and reached for his MP-5.

Bolan squeezed the Walther's trigger, preventing the guard from getting off a shot. The man's knees buckled as he went down like a sack of grain. The bullet had drilled a hole through his forehead to match that of his partner.

Bolan ejected the half-spent magazine from its ammo port, replacing it with a fresh one. He had learned long ago that entering into a new battle without a full load was a foolhardy strategy inviting disaster.

With the immediate danger from the roof sentries neutralized, Bolan squirmed his arms out of the small secondary parachute he had been wearing below his breastbone. Holding the nylon pack in one hand and the Walther in his other, he ran to the west side of the hotel, leaned over the parapet and looked down at the street. Parked at the curb on the alleyway running behind the hotel, almost directly below him, was a red Porsche Boxster with gray interior, its convertible top down.

Bolan placed the small parachute on the rooftop against the parapet with the shoulder straps pointing out. While performing a touch-check on his equipment, he turned and began walking toward the roof's access door. When he reached it, his expectation that the door would be locked with a heavy dead bolt was confirmed. Someone as paranoid as McCarthy, who would purchase five complete floors below his to keep invaders away, could not be expected to allow easy access to his penthouse from above.

Bolan holstered his Walther and reached into the pouch on his web belt containing the incendiary tape. Using his knife, he cut a strip from the roll and wedged it into the crack between the door and frame where he could see the dead bolt. With his knife's blade, he jammed the tape into place, creating as much contact as possible between the material and the metal bolt. Once the tape was secure, he put the remainder of the roll back into its pouch and withdrew a small tube containing a substance resembling petroleum jelly. With the tip of his knife, he pierced the tube and smeared a generous dollop into the crack over the tape.

The tape's active ingredient was a waxy allotrope of white phosphorus that CIA scientists had altered to retard the chemical's natural reaction to oxygen in the atmosphere, thus making it a portable product. The goop in the tube was a sodium-based oxidant that would react in approximately thirty seconds with the willy peter in the tape, bringing it to a flash point hundreds of degrees hotter than what was needed to burn through hardened steel.

Once the tape was coated, Bolan averted his eyes while standing close to the door to hide the quick flash that would occur when the tape ignited. The phosphorus buzzed for an instant before bursting into a white-hot exothermic flame that produced a glow similar to that of an acetylene torch. The burn-through was quick, taking less than ten seconds for the incendiary tape to slice cleanly through the locked dead bolt. Bolan touched the door frame, finding it too hot from heat transference to grab. Using his combat knife as a lever, he pulled the edge toward him. A thin tendril of white smoke curled skyward as the door swung open on silent hinges.

The rooftop access door led to a narrow stairway with cinder-block walls. Bolan drew his pistols, and with the Walther in one hand and his Desert Eagle in the other, he quickly descended the first twelve stairs to a small landing from which twelve additional steps continued down at a right angle. Before he went farther, Bolan holstered his Desert Eagle and inspected the point where the beams supporting the stair frame were bolted into the cinder blocks. The construction was sturdy but old, a condition he tucked into the back of his mind. Prior to moving on, he took the time to wrap the leftover incendiary tape around the supporting bolts. When he was out of tape, he drew the Desert Eagle and finished descending the stairs.

At the bottom of the stairwell he found a wooden door with a small window at eye level. There was no lock on the door. The fact that the stairway ended meant there was another exit stairway somewhere in the penthouse apartment providing egress to the floors below McCarthy's. When the fighting broke out, reinforcements would come up those stairs or off the elevator. It was important that Bolan locate both as quickly as possible.

He peered through the corner of the window into a living space reminiscent of a hunting lodge. Walls and a soaring cathedral ceiling were finished in a wide-planked tongue-in-groove wood, stained a light blond color to accentuate the grain. Oriental rugs were strewed throughout, covering dark hardwood floors. Except for a closed-off bedroom in a distant corner, the floor plan was completely open. In place of load-bearing walls, thick wooden posts twice the diameter of telephone poles provided support for the spacious apartment. Furniture and appliance groupings defined functionality.

Immediately inside the door, an entertainment area

extended for at least fifty feet in each direction. Leather couches and matching love seats, expensive-looking occasional tables and various upholstered chairs were arranged in clusters. A gigantic flat-screen television was mounted on one wall halfway between Bolan and an area containing kitchen appliances, cupboards and freestanding butcher block islands with granite countertops.

Two guards sat on a long leather couch watching a boxing match that played ten times larger than life on the high-definition screen, their MP-5 machine guns leaning barrel-up against chairs within easy reach. Bolan noticed that like the guards on the roof, their short weapons were equipped with sound suppressors. Extending from the ammo port of each, he could see curved magazines capable of holding thirty 9 mm rounds.

Bolan took a deep breath, grabbed the doorknob with the same hand holding the small Walther, and opened the door. He was three steps inside the apartment before one of the guards looked up, saw the intruder's black clothes and painted face, and immediately realized he wasn't one of their own. The two men reacted together, jumping for their MP-5s as if they were performing a choreographed move they had practiced hundreds of times.

Bolan dived to the side, pulling the PPK's trigger as he flew through the air. Three rounds hit one of the guards lunging for his weapon, killing him before he hit the floor where the blood gushing from his wounds flowed into an ugly pattern onto the expensive Persian rug. His action unwittingly shielded his partner, who successfully reached his MP-5 and swung it in Bolan's direction, the barrel spitting 9 mm death on full-auto. With the suppressor attached, the submachine gun sounded like a sputtering faucet, spraying lethal lead across the room inches to both sides of Bolan's head as he crouched behind one of the thick supporting beams. With slugs impacting the walls behind him, Bolan released the magazine from the Walther, reached into his ammo pouch for a fresh one and rammed it home.

"Attack! We're being attacked!" the guard shouted at the top of his lungs, competing to be heard above the sound of the boxing match blaring out from the television.

Knowing the battle was about to get considerably worse before it got better, Bolan waited for the guard to exhaust his 30-round magazine so he could make his move. When he felt the momentary pause he knew indicated an ammo change, he dashed out from behind his cover, the Desert Eagle blazing as he worked the trigger for all he was worth. The heavy handgun's throaty roar shook the apartment with the deafening sounds of combat. The guard scrambled for cover behind the couch, but leather cushions were no match for the .44 Magnum slugs pouring from Bolan's handgun. The bullets ripped through the furniture and found their mark, wounding the man. He continued firing his weapon in Bolan's direction from a spot somewhere on the floor out of sight behind the tattered couch.

Bolan sprinted down the side of the room toward the kitchen area. When he got halfway there, he could see around the edge of the couch. The injured guard was looking away, completely unaware that his adversary had outflanked him. Without slowing his dash to a place that would give him cover as well as a panoramic view of the room, Bolan informed his enemy of his new position by sending him a message in .44 Magnum lead.

Two hefty slugs, fired so close together their retorts seemed to merge into one, struck the man in the neck, all but decapitating him with their awesome force. A scarlet geyser shot forth from the man's shredded carotid artery, dousing the back of what was once a very expensive couch.

Bolan heard the first sounds of reinforcements as they streamed into the room from a short hallway containing a stairwell. Four came into view all at once, their MP-5s on full-auto as they hosed the wide open room indiscriminately with a hail of bullets. Hot lead zipped and cut the air, shattering the HD television screen into jagged shards that fell to the floor in a glittering waterfall. Some of the weapons were not outfitted with suppressors, and the sound of gunfire reached a crescendo with bullets ricocheting off furniture, metal lamps and electronic gear, whining with ear-splitting screams as the rounds skipped across the kitchen's granite countertops.

From his covered spot behind a butcher-block island, Bolan returned fire. The front gunman came charging forward, his assault rifle held low, and Bolan peppered him with rounds from both his weapons. The combination of .38 and .44 slugs twisted and turned the victim in a grotesque death dance before he crumpled to the floor.

The remaining three guards began working as a unit, attempting to dash along the outside walls under the cover of a teammate's fire. Their actions were poorly coordinated, and Bolan was able to concentrate on one at a time. He plugged the man who seemed to be shouting orders to the other two as soon as he rose from behind a supporting beam, sending a stream of lead from the Desert Eagle into him. The volley picked him off his feet, throwing him back to the edge of the hallway where he shimmied for an instant on the polished hardwood floor before succumbing to massive internal damage.

The remaining duo decided to throw everything they had at the intruder. Without concern for anything except volume, they fired at Bolan's position, exhausting one 30-round clip after another, filling the air with lead so thick a passing housefly could not have survived the cross fire. The cabinets above Bolan exploded into wooden slivers that thickened the air with a coarse sawdust. He remained behind the sturdy hardwood island, his handguns at the ready with fresh magazines.

Silence abruptly settled over the battlefield.

"Mr. McCarthy!" one of the two remaining guards called out. "You okay?"

"Yeah!" a voice came from behind the closed bedroom door. "You get him?"

The guards didn't answer.

"Did you get him, goddammit!" McCarthy screamed.

"I don't know!" the guard answered.

The two men crouched behind supporting beams approximately twenty feet apart, fifty feet away from Bolan. From one of his pouches, he pulled a concussion grenade, removed the safety pin and tossed the apple-shaped bomb on a trajectory between the two. As the grenade rolled away from him, he covered his ears and pressed himself into the back of the island giving him cover. The orb bounced a little on the carpet, but the roll remained true, reaching a spot between them when the TNT detonated with an eardrum-throbbing force that shook the entire room.

When the explosive package detonated, it punched the two remaining guards with the force of a hundred sledgehammers. Across the apartment, the door to the bedroom was blown clean off its hinges.

"McCarthy!" Bolan shouted into the chaos. "Come out with your hands up."

He waited for a few seconds before adding, "If I come get you, you'll wish you came out. Let's deal."

"Okay, okay!" McCarthy yelled back, his voice conveying his terror.

He stepped out of the room, his hands held over his head.

"Who are you?" he demanded, looking wildly around the room.

Bolan stood, his pistols in both hands. "Is there anyone else in there?"

"No. No, there's not. But you're not getting away with this. You may kill me, but you're going down, too. Reinforcements are on their way. You'll never leave this hotel alive."

Bolan stepped out from behind the island and began walking toward McCarthy, passing through what looked like the aftermath of a tornado. The stink of death hung heavy from the six corpses littering the apartment.

"Never," McCarthy repeated, staring down the barrels of Bolan's hardware. Recognition dawned on his face, and he said, "Couldn't we have struck a deal? Did it have to come to this?"

"Your choice," Bolan replied, keeping his weapons centered on the crime boss. "I just came to get my gun back."

McCarthy exhaled a short huff that almost sounded like a chuckle, and motioned with his head to a table a few feet from the bedroom doorway. The Beretta sat where he had tossed it earlier that day, having miraculously escaped the firestorm that destroyed almost everything else in the room. Without removing his eyes from McCarthy, Bolan took a few steps to the table and switched the Beretta for the Walther, leaving the PPK on the table where the 93-R had been. The mechanical indicator on the side of the Beretta told Bolan there was a round chambered. When he picked it up, he knew the magazine was full, as it had been when McCarthy took the weapon from him.

"Now," he said, pointing the Beretta at McCarthy's legs, "this appears to be ready to go. I can test it out on your legs and move up until I run out of bullets, or you can tell me what I want to know."

For all his bravado, McCarthy was scared. Bolan could sense his terror the way a dog could sense a person's fear. The crime boss looked away for a second and licked his lips, perhaps calculating his odds.

"The drop is tomorrow morning," he said flatly. "In Spain."

Without a doubt, Bolan thought, McCarthy was telling the truth.

"Spain? It's a big country," he said.

"Our contact, the Piaseczna woman, told Koko to check in to the Sheraton in Madrid. She was going to contact him and set up the drop."

"Koko. Your bodyguard?"

McCarthy nodded. "He flew out of Vegas shortly after you left our place."

"Who does Koko give it to?"

McCarthy chewed on his bottom lip for a second, apparently weighing whether or not to be square with Bolan.

"Right now. The whole story or you die," Bolan said through clenched teeth.

McCarthy lowered his hands and shrugged. "We're killing her and delivering the package to a post-office box in Paris."

"Classy," Bolan said.

McCarthy smirked, said, "Her customer contacted us after she told them we'd be the ones delivering the goods. They were going to kill her anyway. Why not us capitalize on the opportunity?"

"Who's the final customer?"

McCarthy shook his head while answering. "Don't know yet, but I will in a day or so. It doesn't really matter, but I like to know who we're doing business with. He wired two million as he was told to, we kill the girl and drop off the package in Paris. End of story."

Bolan began backing away, keeping his eyes and weapons trained on McCarthy. He was mulling whether or not to kill the man in cold blood when the stairwell door in the hallway burst open and two men came running, assault rifles at the ready.

With his fingers moving in a blur, Bolan thumbed the fire indicator above the Beretta's trigger guard to the tri-burst position and let loose with a 3-round volley at the same time he launched himself through the air toward a spot behind one of the supporting beams. Simultaneous with his move, McCarthy lunged toward the PPK sitting on the table.

Bolan loosed another 3-round burst at the guards while repeatedly firing his Desert Eagle into McCarthy's torso where the heavy rounds stitched a line in Magnum lead. When they exited the body, they opened holes the size of a prizefighter's fist, splashing the wall outside his bedroom with a bloody spray.

With both his weapons in hand, Bolan engaged the less experienced guards. Although they possessed greater potential firepower with the MP-5 submachine guns, they lacked the combat experience of their opponent, who was able to use the chaos inherent in a firefight to his advantage. The guards were intent on hosing down the area around Bolan's post with 9 mm lead. Such a tactic, while terrifying for the uninitiated, accomplished little in terms of actually killing their target.

Bolan remained low. A break came from the gunman

on the left, and Bolan leaped from his position like a sprinter exploding out of the blocks. With his Desert Eagle pounding out potential death, he sprinted toward another post in the direction of his enemy on the right, pulling the trigger of his oversize handgun as quickly as he could in order to keep the man from returning fire.

The gunman on the right peeked out from the corner of the wooden supporting beam he was hiding behind, exposing less than a quarter of his face. It was all Bolan needed as he dashed toward the door he had come through when he first entered the apartment. His powerful rounds tore through the corner of the wooden post, splintering a chunk and making it look as if someone had taken a bite out of the wooden column. The round continued on its course, slamming into the man's right eye and throwing him ten feet toward the hallway where he landed on top of one of the corpses that had been deposited there during the initial firefight.

Finding himself within sprinting distance of the door leading to the roof, Bolan hugged the post, giving him cover while he changed the magazines in his weapons. He had known all along he was going to get his Beretta back, and had come with extra 9 mm rounds loaded into two clips. Checking to make sure that the fire selector was still set for 3-round bursts, he prepared for his escape.

Bolan heard the arrival of new reinforcements, who upon seeing the incredible devastation in the apartment, immediately assumed prone positions in the hallway. Although they possessed numbers as well as weapons superiority, they had apparently decided to enter with caution.

Bolan knew the lone enemy he was presently engaging would be momentarily distracted by the arrival of reinforcements, and he seized the opportunity to make his escape. With the Beretta spitting 3-round bursts, and the Desert Eagle thumping out .44-caliber slugs, Bolan made a dash for the roof stairway, getting through the door and slamming it closed behind him in a hail of bullets that came within a finger's width of his head.

He raced up the stairs while pulling his final concussion grenade from the pouch on his web belt. He set the fuse for thirty seconds and left the bomb sitting on the first landing as he ran out the door to the roof. Sprinting over the pebbly surface for all he was worth, he reached the spot where he had placed the smaller version of his arrival parachute.

His weapons were securely holstered, and his arms were halfway into the chute's straps when the grenade detonated with a force sufficient to ignite the incendiary tape he had wrapped around the stairway's supporting bolts. Between the willy peter and the grenade's formidable shock wave, the staircase separated from the cinder-block wall, crumpling into a twisted mass of hot metal. A medley of anguished cries and angry curses told him the stairwell had not been deserted when the bomb went off.

After tugging the straps tight, Bolan stepped up onto the precipice and launched himself off the top of the building into the night air. Assuming a flat-out posture, he watched the ground approach. At the fortieth story, he tightened his grip on the rip cord handle. At twenty floors up, he pulled the cord.

The miniature chute popped open, jerking the straps into his armpits. With its reduced area, the chute's deceleration ability was extremely limited, and Bolan hit the ground with a force equivalent to that encountered by jumping from a platform roughly fifteen-feet high. He rolled upon hitting the ground to absorb some of the shock, but his teeth were rattled as he tore off his chute and jumped into the waiting Porsche Boxster.

The automobile was loaded with electronic gear Akira Tokaido had programmed. The powerful engine jumped to life as soon as Bolan's fingers touched the steering wheel, revving with all the impatience of a prized Thoroughbred at the starting gate. Bolan threw the transmission into gear, stomped the accelerator, and the car took off like a rocket alongside the back of the hotel as half a dozen men with automatic rifles came pouring out the front door.

With the high-performance tires squealing in protest, Bolan negotiated the corners behind the hotel, coming out onto Mandalay Bay Road in a sideways skid. Fighting the steering wheel while he accelerated, he pulled the sports car out of its slide and onto Frank Sinatra Drive going south. In his rearview mirror, Bolan could see the headlights of a car leaving the hotel parking lot at a high speed and knew it was McCarthy's men.

The entrance ramp to Route 15 South was straight ahead, and Bolan floored the gas pedal. The headlights behind him became smaller and smaller as the Boxster's speedometer climbed steadily from 100 to 120, to 150, to 180. The highway was wide, straight and flat, stretching without so much as a curve for the next 265 miles to San Diego, and Bolan had no problem whatsoever handling the high-performance machine through its rapid acceleration.

When the headlights vanished from rearview sight, he touched a switch on the outside of the steering wheel.

"Yeah, Striker," Mitch Davidson's voice came over the high-fidelity speakers as clearly as if the pilot was sitting in the plush leather seat next to him.

"South on 15. Where are you?"

"Roger. Got you. Roadway's clear ahead."

"Do it fast. I'm about a minute ahead of McCarthy's guys."

The C-21A Learjet swooped low over the Boxster, touching down on the highway as soon as it cleared the car. It was traveling at about 250 miles per hour, and continued to distance itself from the car even as Davidson applied the brakes. After about thirty seconds, the relative velocities were reversed, and the Porsche caught up to the airplane just as the customized cargo ramp was lowering.

Bolan touched the brakes, slowing the car from a speed in excess of 160 down to fifty, which was the fastest he dared drive into the plane's cargo port. The back tires were barely inside when the ramp began closing and the jet accelerated.

Takeoff was smooth, and the plane was out of sight a full ten seconds before the speeding sedan carrying the remnants of McCarthy's army came over the horizon whizzing south on Route 15.

At thirty thousand feet, Bolan called Brognola on a secure line.

"The drop is somewhere in Spain, scheduled for tomorrow morning."

"Somewhere in Spain is not very specific."

"Best we have. Kohotina is picking it up and taking it to Paris.

"Paris is a big city."

"See you at the Farm," Bolan said and hung up.

7

Pamplona, Spain

Early, before the mist burned off and revelers filled the streets, Pamplona was soft. Even the Plaza de Toros in the center of town—garish at noon, when arterial spillings vied for brilliance with the gaudy bunting that drapes the stadium like multicolored tinsel on a Christmas tree—at that hour was a study in pastels.

Marlene Piaseczna turned her face to the morning sun. She savored the ambiance, sensing it would be short-lived. Sparrows hopped close, pecking microscopic morsels from between mortar joints in the brick floor, their satisfied chirps blending with the tinkling of silverware being set on tables nearby. The air smelled clean and wet.

She closed her eyes, breathing deeply. Soon, she would have more money than she had ever dreamed possible. And the jerks back at Nautech Corporation could take that engineering job and shove it where the sun didn't shine. All that talk about teamwork and the value of diversity. She had bought into it at first, but in the end it was nothing but talk. When push came to shove, the place was nothing but a boys' club. Smart women need not apply. She had come to wonder if, when they had hired her, they had ever been interested in her mind.

A waiter appeared at her table, scrutinizing her the way men had eyed her since high school. As much as Marlene hated being judged on the basis of her looks, she had used them to her advantage ever since she had realized she could.

"I'd like a liter of your sangria, please," she ordered in Spanish.

The waiter's eyebrows shot up.

"Is it too early?"

"Oh, no, miss. During the festivals, there is neither too early nor too late," he replied.

"What is it, then?"

He hesitated, embarrassed. "Are you Pamplonan, miss? My ears say you are, but I know our families."

"Many people speak Spanish," she replied, her shining green eyes dancing in a way that made his heart skip.

He wagged a finger as if to scold. "Spanish, yes. Pamplonan, no."

Her smile made the waiter wish he was single and twenty years younger.

"You do me honor, sir," she said in perfect dialect. "No, I'm not from your beautiful city, but I visit often."

He bowed politely. "For you, my lady, I will bring our best."

He moved off, stopping to seat other customers. During the quarterly festivals, cafés along the route filled hours before the actual running, almost as quickly as they did during the world-famous San Fermin.

A pounding noise floated up from the street, and Marlene stood to look beyond the restraining rails encircling the café's balcony. On the cobblestone street below, two policemen argued while adjusting a brightly painted barricade. They pulled the six-foot-high wooden barrier into place, gave it a few whacks with a rubber sledge and, still bickering, walked off to inspect the next intersection. Their work would be tested in a few hours.

Before sitting, Marlene leaned over the railing to get a better look at the route the bulls would run.

JOHNNY KOHOTINA WAS suddenly awake, instantly alert. He knew it was six o'clock without having to look. The world was very different for him on contract days. This day, he would kill.

Kohotina had made his bones for the McCarthy Family more than two decades earlier when he was an angry high-school dropout with limited skills. He had shown up in Las Vegas one step ahead of the Hawaiian authorities pursuing him on a rape charge, and had been happy for the opportunity Michael McCarthy, who was always on the lookout for violent talent, offered him. Over the years, his willingness to kill—and to do it slowly or quickly as the boss directed—enabled him to progress through the ranks, eventually becoming McCarthy's personal bodyguard. In was in this position, while defending his boss in a manner that the district attorney was able to convince a jury had not required the deadly force he applied, that led to his five-year break in service. During the resulting time at San Quentin, the Family had remained true, and he returned from a sentence during which none of the other inmates dared bother him.

Kohotina rolled onto the floor and dragged a suitcase from under the bed. From behind a false panel in the luggage, he withdrew a .22-caliber pistol. He handled the weapon the way an antique dealer might hold a valuable work of porcelain—firmly and comfortably, but with great respect. It was a Ruger Mark II, semiautomatic pistol, no serial number. It had taken him hours to rebore the barrel and adapt the sights for a sound suppressor, but when he finished, he was confident he had crafted a perfect tool. It was important for him to know his weapons the way a photographer knew film, or a sculptor stone. A true artist loved not only his work, but also the medium.

Kohotina glanced at his watch for the first time since awakening. His skills would be tested in a few hours.

BY SEVEN O'CLOCK, Marlene was feeling a trifle drunk. It was early to be drinking, but since things were going so perfectly according to plan, she didn't feel the need to hold back. The previous night she had staked out the hotel a few blocks away where she told McCarthy's guy to check in when he called from Madrid to get details for their meeting. From the description he had given, she was sure it was the big Hawaiian guy who arrived around six o'clock. She had toyed with the idea of going to the bar and seeing if she could pick him up for what she suspected might be some torrid sex, but decided in the end to keep everything professional. He was scheduled to meet her here in about an hour, at which point she'd give him the envelope in her purse in return for a thick package of money to cover her short-term expenses. After what she had been put through at that testosterone-crazed factory in San Diego, Marlene figured she had earned the right to celebrate a little.

In a fleeting moment of reflection, Marlene wondered how many sailors would be killed when ADAS went down and terrorists were able to attack an unprotected aircraft carrier. The system's failure to do what it had been designed to do would be traced back to Nautech, of course, and the company would get exactly what it deserved. Maybe they'd even be banned from doing future defense work. How sweet would that be?

Even with the risk of prosecution, Marlene hoped some of the managers would make the link between her and the disaster. She'd be invisible in another week or so, looking for someplace in Europe where her language skills would enable her to blend into the general population. But it would be gratifying to know that the men at Nautech realized the outcast they had mocked and made fun of was responsible for their company's downfall.

Her friends had been outcasts, too. Brilliant engineers, highly motivated when they'd first started at Nautech. But the company's bullying culture, where rude, aggressive behavior was rewarded, had ground them all down. The only thing they could fight back with was their intelligence. Once they'd decided to exact revenge on the company, they had easily stolen the code right off the system while it was undergoing final integration and prove-out in the test lab. It was a shame they wouldn't be able to share in the spoils of their success. In retrospect, Marlene realized they should have known a terrorist couldn't be trusted.

With a slight shudder, she thought for at least the thousandth time since learning through the Internet about the brutal murders of three engineers in Manitoba that it could have been her, too. It was only by chance that her grandfather, who had been in a vegetative state in a nursing home for more than two years, picked the very day before the attack on the cabin to die. His funeral was all that had kept her from being with her friends on that fateful day.

She pushed the depressing thought from her head and raised her hand, bringing the waiter immediately to her side.

"Not another liter, miss? Are you sure?"

"I'm sure."

"You will miss the Encierro," he said in French.

Marlene laughed. "I have seen them run before," she responded to his game.

She had been one of the smartest in her class at MIT, entering as a freshman with dual majors. A double major was somewhat of a rarity at the Cambridge institute that prided itself on proving to high-school geniuses how difficult a curriculum leading to a single degree could be. Marlene's second major had been modern European languages. She went to Boston fluent in three; when she left for San Diego four years later with a degree in mathematics, she was speaking seven.

"Ah!" the waiter replied, switching to English. "Even tipsy, you speak better French than I. Mademoiselle is Parisian, *oui?* So cultured and refined?"

"Where we're from is meaningless," she answered with a slight slur. "Where we are going is all that matters."

The waiter sighed theatrically. "You are a wonderful enigma, my beauty, but dreamland is the only place you are going. But do not worry. If you require assistance, I will escort you safely to your room. My only reward—" his eyes twinkled "—will be your nationality."

"Deal!" Marlene said enthusiastically.

The waiter departed, leaving her to her thoughts. She swirled the remaining wine in the bottom of her glass, raised it in a mock toast.

"To you, John Moorhead," she said quietly, "may we never meet again."

Marlene learned a lot about men in general and John Moorhead in particular when she went to work in his software engineering department at Nautech.

At first she liked everything about him. He seemed sincere, able to talk the talk with the best of them. But when it came time for promotions and achievement awards, it was Moorhead's inner clique that always got the recognition. Marlene had talked to Human Resources about her perception that performance wasn't being rewarded like everyone said it was, but rather than correcting the problem, the HR guy went straight to Moorhead to tell him he had a dissenter on his team.

Life after that became unbearable, with Moorhead watching her every move, never missing an opportunity to criticize and belittle her actions. The entire team followed his lead, making her feel like an outsider by demanding more and more of her while letting their inner group slide. When Moorhead's buddies started referring to her by parts of the female anatomy, she knew she had to get out of there. But she wasn't about to leave poor, that was for sure.

The sound of a rocket broke through her thoughts. Marlene looked up and saw the waiter approaching with her wine.

"One hour," he said in English as he placed the carafe on her table. "Did you hear the chupinazo?"

"I did," she answered. "I'm very impressed with your languages."

He shrugged, blushing slightly. "Three is all. But it's mostly all I need. Someday I'll learn German, but they don't come here often enough."

Marlene poured wine into her glass with shaky hands. *"Danke."* She smiled.

"No, no, my lady," he said, laughing as he walked away, "do not try to say you are German. You are much too cultured to be German."

Marlene leaned back in her chair and closed her

eyes. The sun was warm, the wine good, the waiter fun. She was beginning to relax.

SITTING AT A TABLE in the restaurant's corner, staring blankly over a glass of tonic water, Kohotina mentally reviewed his plan. From his spot, he could see his target across the crowded outdoor café. He'd make the deal, get the software and give her the money. He'd limit their chitchat to a minimum; there was no possible upside to lingering. As a parting gift when he left, he'd give her a .22-caliber hollowpoint round to the head.

Having done jobs like this before, killing in public didn't faze Kohotina in the least. To him, it was all about confidence and misdirection. He knew that when properly done, a professional could pop someone in plain sight, and not one bystander would remember enough to be a good witness.

He inhaled fully through his nose, paused and slowly blew out through pursed lips. The technique was a relaxation method he had learned in prison. For the well-protected, San Quentin had been like a trade school with professionals passing the benefits of lessons to younger inmates. As Kohotina continued to breathe, waves of energy began pulsing through his body. He visualized the oxygen spreading outward from his lungs, racing into his bloodstream and down his right arm, to his hand playing over the weapon in his jacket pocket.

THE WAITER STOPPED BY Marlene's table as a soft breeze carried the sound of a cannon to her ears. The first bulls had been set loose to begin their stampede through the streets.

"Are you all right, my beautiful one?"

"I'm fine." She smiled.

"Your eyes say they have had their fill of wine."

"Don't listen to my eyes."

"Be careful if you go to watch the Encierro." He motioned to the railing above the street.

"I'm not," Marlene answered. "I'm happy here."

Recalling her last visit to Pamplona when she had witnessed a runner being fatally gored during the stampede, she asked, "Do you think there will be deaths today?"

"There always are," the waiter replied, shaking his head as he began moving away. "Death runs with the herd. We will find its work when the bulls have passed."

An overweight man with a camera slung from his sweating neck bumped Marlene's table, and she grabbed her glass and the carafe to prevent them from spilling. As the table settled, she noticed a pattern of movement from the corner of her eye. Her contact was approaching, causing her heartbeat to accelerate. It was happening—she was about to close the deal. Her fallen friends flashed through her mind, and she felt a stab of sorrow that their lives had been lost, preventing them from being there to experience victory with her. It couldn't have been foreseen, but it should not have gone down that way. The four of them should have ended up happy together in the Caymans.

"Hello," the man said, sliding into the chair next to Marlene. "It's a beautiful day for a bullfight."

"More beautiful than Mexico ever gets," she replied, completing the phrase they had agreed upon over the phone.

"Do you have it?" Kohotina asked.

He was momentarily taken aback by the beauty he had not appreciated from a distance. The top two buttons of the woman's blouse were open, exposing a generous portion of a bright green bra that played to the color of her eyes. Her short blond hair sparkled in the morning sun, framing a petite, doll-like face. She was, without question, a stunning young woman.

Under different circumstances, Kohotina might rethink his plan. A prize like this could be taken to a remote location where he'd delight himself for hours before killing her. But he had called Las Vegas late the previous night and been told that McCarthy and most of his troops were dead. Kohotina wasn't sure what that meant specifically for him, but he thought it was important for him to finish this mission. If the Family was being thrown into turmoil, it didn't need a dissatisfied customer who had already sent them two million bucks thinking they wouldn't fulfill their part of the contract.

In answer to his question, Marlene slid a square envelope across the table.

"There are two CDs and a flash drive here. It's all they need."

He scooped them up, placed them in his jacket's inner breast pocket and buttoned the flap closed. Reaching into his pants pocket, he pulled out a business-sized envelope strained to the limit by its contents.

"Twenty grand," he said, speaking over the noise of the stampeding bulls below. "The party money you asked for."

The front-running bulls from a second group that had been released from their pens on the other side of town were just reaching the roadway below.

Marlene reached for the envelope as Kohotina stood, his hand concealed inside his jacket.

Half the people jammed against the safety railing shouted encouragement to the runners below, while the other half hurled insults at the stampeding bulls as if the animals could understand their drunken slurs. The

NO POSTAGE
NECESSARY
IF MAILED
IN THE
UNITED STATES

BUSINESS REPLY MAIL
FIRST-CLASS MAIL   PERMIT NO. 717   BUFFALO, NY

POSTAGE WILL BE PAID BY ADDRESSEE

GOLD EAGLE READER SERVICE
3010 WALDEN AVE
PO BOX 1867
BUFFALO NY 14240-9952

Get FREE BOOKS and a FREE GIFT when you play the...

LAS VEGAS
GAME

*Just scratch off
the gold box with a coin.
Then check below to see
the gifts you get!*

YES! I have scratched off the gold box. Please send me my **2 FREE BOOKS** and **gift for which I qualify.** I understand that I am under no obligation to purchase any books as explained on the back of this card.

▼ DETACH AND MAIL CARD TODAY! ▼

366 ADL ENWS

166 ADL ENX4
(GE-LV-08)

FIRST NAME	LAST NAME

ADDRESS

APT.#	CITY

STATE/PROV.	ZIP/POSTAL CODE

7	7	7	Worth TWO FREE BOOKS plus a BONUS Mystery Gift!
🍒	🍒	🍒	Worth TWO FREE BOOKS!
🔔	🔔	♣	TRY AGAIN!

Offer limited to one per household and not valid to current subscribers of Gold Eagle® books. All orders subject to approval. Please allow 4 to 6 weeks for delivery.

Your Privacy - Worldwide Library is committed to protecting your privacy. Our privacy policy is available online at www.eHarlequin.com or upon request from the Gold Eagle Reader Service. From time to time we make our lists of customers available to reputable third parties who may have a product or service of interest to you. If you would prefer for us not to share your name and address, please check here.☐

high degree of intoxication among all in attendance contributed significantly to the confusion and absolute pandemonium.

Kohotina took a few steps away from the table before turning back as if he had forgotten something. When he extended his hand the way he would to stroke the side of a lover's face in farewell, it contained the small Ruger.

Marlene smiled and leaned forward, assuming her visitor was about to caress her cheek. The thought that maybe she and the big guy could link up back at the hotel flashed through her mind, immediately followed by the realization that there was a gun in his hand. Her eyes widened in terror, and a scream that never got the nanosecond it needed to reach her lips formed in her throat.

As he had visualized, Kohotina extended the pistol to arm's length and fired twice, the light .22-caliber pops lost in the noise produced by the stampeding herd below. From mere inches away, the barrel spewed hot gases and ammo residue, causing Marlene's flawless skin to blister with powder burns. The Ruger's hollow-point rounds flattened upon impact, blowing most of the young woman's extremely intelligent brain tissue out the back of her head. She fell back in her chair, her beautiful eyes staring dull and sightless into the morning sky.

The herd passed, and a woman's screams brought the waiter running. He looked to where the hysterical woman pointed, and saw Marlene. She was slumped in the chair, with blood trickling from a messy head wound down her face and around her neck into the cleavage framed by her pretty green bra.

The waiter stared at her body, unable to move. Someone finally grabbed and shook him, and he ran to call the police. By the time they arrived on the scene,

Kohotina was almost back to his hotel, idly wondering how the call girls in Paris would measure up to what he was used to getting in Las Vegas.

8

Hal Brognola dealt half a dozen eight-by-ten color photographs onto the conference table for all to see. "My God, Striker," he said, shaking his head. "Could you have done more damage out there?" He was sitting across from the Executioner in the War Room at Stony Man Farm.

"He took my Beretta, Hal," Bolan replied with a false innocence that brought a smile to the corners of Carmen Delahunt's mouth.

"Yo." Tokaido endorsed Bolan's explanation, snapping his bubble gum while nodding his head in time to the rock music streaming through his earbuds.

"Can't let a man take your gun," Delahunt said, noticing that Wethers was nodding in agreement as well.

Wethers had done some research that convinced him something big was brewing with one of the fundamentalist militias dedicated to jihad against the West. Increased phone traffic, money transfers and satellite surveillance showing nighttime troop and equipment movement in three towns just across the Iraqi border in Iran led him to believe he was witnessing a staging operation. If this was the same group trying to buy the ADAS code, Wethers expected the situation would get a lot worse before it got any better. Unfortunately for the safety of the men and women serving on the aircraft carriers in the Persian Gulf, a preemptive strike into Iran was not a strategy the President could be expected to embrace.

Before their conversation concerning Bolan's techniques in Las Vegas progressed further, Barbara Price and Aaron Kurtzman entered the room. Brognola reached out and scooped up the photos, arranging the glossy images into a neat stack before slipping them into a thin leather folder he kept on the table in front of him.

Stony Man Farm's mission controller got right to business while Kurtzman wheeled himself to the vacant spot at the head of the table.

"Spain," Price said, sliding into the chair next to Delahunt. "Where do we stand? The drop is today?"

"That's what McCarthy said," Bolan answered, "and I believe it."

Kurtzman's group had been working around the clock since the moment Bolan called Brognola from the jet over Route 15 in Las Vegas to share the information he had obtained from McCarthy. So far, their strategy to scan airport and financial databases in an attempt to locate Marlene Piaseczna had met with complete failure. In spite of their hard work, no one on the cybernetics team had been able to uncover so much as a scrap of evidence indicating she was in Europe.

Brognola spoke up, studying his fingernails while he said, "We know for sure that Johnny Kohotina, McCarthy's personal bodyguard, passed through Spanish customs at the Madrid airport late yesterday. Spain is six hours ahead of us. If what McCarthy told Striker is true, the drop has already taken place."

"It's just too big of a country," Price said with a sigh. "Even with us knowing he flew into Madrid, we simply don't have a lot to go on. His entire trip there could be nothing more than a red herring."

"I believed McCarthy," Bolan repeated.

"Then that means the code is probably on its way to Paris," Delahunt said.

"Or already there." It was Wethers who voiced the scenario none of them wanted to hear. Directing his gaze at Brognola, he asked, "Any word from Interpol that he's in France?"

The man from Justice shook his head slowly. "There are too many ways for him to get in from Spain. If he flies under his own passport into one of the Paris airports, there's a good chance he'll get picked up. But if he goes by train or car, or if he takes a tour bus or something…" His voice tapered off before he stated the obvious.

"He probably checked in with his people at some point," Delahunt said into the silence that settled over the group as the realization that the code was most likely on its way to a terrorist organization sunk in. "So he knows that his boss and a bunch of his soldiers were killed. That would put him into a defensive mode. He's not going to fly into one of the Paris airports."

Kurtzman took a long sip of his potent coffee, held it in his mouth for a few seconds to savor the flavor before swallowing, then spoke for the first time.

"McCarthy has a warehouse in Paris," he said, looking at one of the notes the team had assembled over the previous twelve hours. "It's logical to assume that Kohotina will go there. Maybe not directly, but eventually he will, don't you think?"

His comment was met by nods from around the table.

"What's the warehouse used for?" Wethers asked, his eyes scanning his teammates for the one who had uncovered the fact and written the note.

"It's a front for opium from Afghanistan," Tokaido spoke up. "The public records I found indicate it's an outlet for designer handbags, but Interpol raided it half a dozen times last year hoping to find drugs. They never did."

"Why do you say opium?" Price asked.

"A flow of money back and forth with businessmen in Kabul. The warehouse is right on the Seine. Easy access in and out."

"Easy as in right on the docks?" Bolan asked.

"You bet."

Price asked, "Where does that leave us? Assume we're correct that Kohotina has already picked up the code and killed Piaseczna. Now his job is to get it to a post office box in Paris. Hal, do we have people watching the post offices over there?"

"We do," Brognola answered, "but there are so many mail drops in the city proper as well as the suburbs that hoping to catch him in the act of mailing it is a real long shot. I think Striker should go to Paris. There's a chance the code hasn't been sent yet to the terrorists. Maybe the deal was for McCarthy to get paid before he mailed it. Maybe Kohotina will try to get more for it now that it's in his possession—especially if he's aware that the guy he was working for isn't around anymore. There are many reasons for him not to have sent the code yet."

Price countered, "And an equal number of reasons why he already has."

"I agree with Hal," Kurtzman said. "We have nothing to lose by sending Striker to Paris."

"And we're all set for Akira going undercover to San Diego?" Brognola asked.

"Yeah," came the chorus of responses.

Bolan sat up straighter in his chair. "Why?"

"Because," Kurtzman broke in before Tokaido could say anything, "Nautech will hire someone with Akira's skills in a second." He was looking directly at Brognola while he spoke, conveying the fact that a discussion between them had preceded the decision. "We understand the downside, believe me. But Robbie Maxwell thought there was a fifth conspirator at the company. Remember the missing million? We've decided to put Akira into the facility for a few weeks to see if he can find out who hung around with Piaseczna. He'll be given appropriate cover. If we can find someone else who was a member of their group, maybe we can find out who's buying the code. Time is running short, Striker. Drastic situations call for drastic action."

Before a discussion rehashing the risks Tokaido would face while going undercover could arise, Price shifted the topic by turning to Wethers and asking, "Hunt, how are you coming on the militia research?"

His report, she knew, would give support to Kurtzman's concerns.

The ex-UC Berkeley professor said, "The situation is not good. First off, let's consider the ambush. It doesn't make sense. I have photos of the soldiers killed in the firefight, taken by the U.S. Army's version of a CSI team."

Reaching into the folder he had brought with him to the meeting, he withdrew two eight-by-ten pictures and slid them down the table to Bolan. "Look at these. The three dead soldiers were found as shown. No sign in the dirt of them scuffling around, no brass littering the area. There are rocks behind them they could have used for cover. Same with the Sunni corpses. And—" he paused for emphasis "—all the dead have ligature marks on their wrists indicating they had been tied up. Do you think a firefight happened here?"

Bolan studied the two pictures for less than ten seconds before saying, "No. This looks like an amateurish attempt to make it appear there was an ambush. Doesn't ring true to me. Even if these two groups bumped into each other they wouldn't just start blasting away. And if two patrols did, they wouldn't die this way. These bodies were posed."

"That's exactly what I thought," Wethers said. "So I asked myself who benefits if we believe the staged attack actually happened. The Sunni dead belonged to the Munjian militia. They're sworn enemies with a number of Shiite groups, among them one called the a'mjuur. I believe they're the ones behind this misdirection. It could be the a'mjuur, not a Sunni group, that's attempting to buy the ADAS code. Planting a small piece on one of the Sunni was intended to mislead us. Buy some time."

He paused and took a sip of water before continuing. "There's more for your consideration," he said, sounding like the professor he had been for most of his life. "U.S. intelligence considers the a'mjuur militia one of the region's most dangerous emerging forces. Rumor has it they hold a significant stockpile of Stinger missiles they obtained from the United States during the Soviet invasion of Afghanistan."

"We gave them Stingers?" Delahunt interrupted. "This militia was around in the eighties?"

"No," Wethers answered, "not directly. Over a nine-year period, the CIA gave the mujahideen guerrillas in Afghanistan more than ten thousand missiles." Anticipating the next question, he shrugged and said, "It was in America's interest during the cold war to keep the Soviets bogged down wherever possible. After communism collapsed, the leftover missiles were dispersed by the mujahideen to regional militias throughout the Middle East. The CIA believes the a'mjuur, commanded by a man named Ali Ansari Hasseim, got a significant number of them."

"Stingers can't take out an aircraft carrier," Price stated.

"Let's say around two pounds of high explosive on the head of a missile is fired from five miles away onto a flight deck where there's fuel tanks, aircraft and tons of ordnance," Bolan said. "Hit the ship with a dozen or so, and she could be in bad shape. How many missiles does the CIA think this militia has?"

"Some estimates put the number as high as fifteen hundred," Wethers replied.

"I have evidence indicating there's a build-up in progress in a few towns around the Strait of Hormuz," he elaborated. "The USS *Eisenhower* is scheduled to sail through the narrow channel around the tip of the Musandam Peninsula sometime within the next two weeks, around the time the USS *Ronald Reagan* will show up to replace her. The timing could not be better. It's a perfect storm."

"Okay," Kurtzman said, "let's assume—"

His words were interrupted by the hum of Brognola's PDA. The big Fed reached into his suit coat's inside pocket and pulled the unit out to read its message.

"Let's assume," Kurtzman continued his thought, "that the militia buying the code capable of disabling ADAS already has a considerable supply of Stinger missiles. What are the steps they take to launch an attack?"

"First they have to download the new code," Tokaido said. "Somehow they'll have to get the new instructions into the hardware already installed onboard the carrier. I'm not sure how they'll do that. It's one of the things I'll learn when I'm at Nautech. Do you have to send someone onto the ship to install the new software into the defense system? I think maybe you do."

"Let's hope you have to," Kurtzman said. "Then what? Once the bogus instructions are loaded, what's next?"

"A coordinated attack," Bolan answered. He was staring into the distance as if he could see the action. "You'd want to strike in an area where the carrier's maneuverability was compromised. Hunt is right. The most vulnerable spot in the Persian Gulf is at the southeast end, where the Strait of Hormuz connects to the Gulf of Oman. You'd want to hit the target from different angles. You could do that from the highlands along the strait."

"Has the Navy been told about this threat?" Price asked, looking at Brognola.

"They have. The President spoke to the secretary, who said every vessel in that region is already on full combat alert. To them this is just one more danger, and there's nothing additional they can do. They're already watching for anything out of the ordinary."

The room fell into a silence that Brognola broke by saying, "Marlene Piaseczna is dead." He motioned to his PDA. "Murdered this morning at an outdoor café in Pamplona."

"An outdoor café in broad daylight?" Price asked.

"During a running of the bulls. All kinds of noise and chaos. No witnesses, although one of the waiters apparently remembers there was a man who was 'kind of big' but nothing else."

"Kohotina," Bolan said.

"Go to Paris and find him," Brognola stated. "Find out if he still has the code he took from that girl. You'll need tools. You can't bring them into France." The big Fed wrote a name and address on a small pad the way a doctor would fill out a prescription. He handed the note to Bolan, who read it once before shoving it into his shirt pocket.

"What about the build-up in the hills above the strait?" the Executioner asked.

"The President has a wing in Oman on strike alert. The problem is that the targets are across the border in Iran. He'll wait until he believes he has absolutely no other alternative before authorizing that one," the big Fed replied.

"Stop Hasseim from getting the other half of the code, Striker," Price said, fixing Bolan with her eyes, "and the President won't have to make that decision."

9

The night ocean was rough, rising in angry waves higher than one hundred feet, listing the aircraft carrier to pitch, roll, swell and turn on four axes that themselves shifted with the seas. A duo of aircraft directors in yellow shirts gave flashlight directions to the blue-shirted plane handlers as the latter guided an F/A-18 Super Hornet into position for takeoff. In addition to using handheld light signals, the directors simultaneously shouted their orders, but they may just as well have been mute, such was the force of the gale winds hammering the USS *Ronald Reagan* with sea spray and drenching rain.

Appearing totally chaotic, the active flight deck of a nuclear-powered aircraft carrier was one of the most intense and hazardous working environments anywhere on Earth. With fighter jets weighing 68,000 pounds accelerating from zero to a takeoff speed of 160 knots in two seconds, with returning aircraft being brought to an abrupt halt within 320 feet of touching the jitterbugging deck, with F/A-18s, radar-equipped E2Cs, antisubmarine S-3s, and SH-34 helicopters being shuttled on massive elevators back and forth from hangar decks to the flight surface, inches and seconds often determine the difference between mission success and catastrophic failure. Each member of the flight crew depended on his shipmates for his safety during a launch and retrieval process that included fifty functional roles. For the team to succeed, every sailor had to know his or her job and perform it to perfection. On the flight deck of an aircraft carrier, there were no small mistakes, no minor injuries. If there was an accident, it was a bad one.

Fighting against the force of hurricane-strength winds pushing them toward the ship's hangar bay, a crew of Grapes—so named for the purple shirts they wore—moved laboriously from one jet to the next in the takeoff queue. Their job was to deliver clear and bright JP-5 aviation fuel to the awaiting aircraft, pumped through heavy orange hoses from the ship's massive 3.9 million gallon reserve tanks.

Lieutenant Artie Mirabillay, the *Reagan*'s top gun, gave a thumbs-up signal to the Grapes on his starboard side when they finished topping off his tank. Blue Shirts guided his aircraft to the bow catapult, and the directors began to process down to takeoff. As the bow cat hurled Mirabillay's fighter jet forward, he opened the plane's throttle, soaring from the deck's slick surface. The flaming exhaust bellowing from his F-18's tailpipe illuminated for a few moments the flight crew's stress-lined faces as they battled the elements hindering their completion of the training mission. Mirabillay gained altitude quickly, climbing above the storm to where the star-studded night sky stretched out before him, peaceful and black. The skilled pilot caressed his fighter's controls, and the aircraft responded with a joyful skip and roll.

Two decks below in the ship's command center, Petty Officer Timothy Bergeron said, "Top gun," with a smile. Watching Mirabillay's maneuver on the ADAS radar screen, he could almost feel the pilot's elation.

Leon Kreamer leaned closer from his seat next to Bergeron. They were alone in the communications center, as was often the case on late watches.

"Mach 1.5. He's moving," Kreamer said.

"Not as fast as he would in a Tomcat. The 18 is a slower plane," Bergeron responded, keeping his eyes on the monitor as ADAS tracked Mirabillay until he moved outside the system's thirty-mile range. The screen was cluttered with symbols representing various aircraft as they performed exercises validating the vessel's seaworthiness.

In quiet times, Bergeron often recalled his grandfather's stories of service on the USS *Midway*. Back then the crew discovered they were about to be attacked when someone with binoculars spotted the first wave of kamikaze Zeros breaking over the horizon heading their way. Now the carriers were much bigger, the F-18s faster, the ordnance they carried so much more destructive and deadly. But the defenses had also kept pace with technology. The *Reagan* was shielded thirty nautical miles out, giving ADAS enough time to run data from the common enterprise communications system at the speed of light through its electronic circuits, match the weapons to the targets and neutralize the threat.

A message abruptly appeared on Bergeron's screen, informing him that a simulation was about to occur.

"Rock and roll," Kreamer said. "You all set?"

Bergeron nodded, rubbing his palms together for a few seconds before placing his fingers into position above the keyboard. His gesture reminded the Nautech engineer of a world-class gymnast getting ready to mount the high bars.

Kreamer thought there was a good chance the ADAS

system's new download capability might be tested this night. Sea trials progressed in random order without repeats, and the *Reagan* had already completed more than eighty percent of the standard tests. Since the system's ability to receive and download new software from an off-site location would be tested, the longer they went without doing it, the more probable it became.

Bergeron's first test did not involve an external threat. ADAS was also connected to the ship's internal communications system, and the first case that came up was a challenge to troubleshoot failing communications between the torpedo hangar and the ship's main engine room. As he read the symptoms describing the failure mode, Bergeron's hands moved back and forth between his operator's console and the command table, opening and closing electronic paths, testing circuits and redirecting communications. He had barely reestablished commo when a missile came speeding toward the ship from the third quadrant. The identification tag labeled its approach at Mach 2—twice the speed of sound.

According to sea-trial rules, Kreamer was allowed to help Bergeron only on specific cases explicitly spelled out ahead of time in his ship rider contract. For the current tests, he was onboard the *Reagan* to offer troubleshooting assistance as required with radar interface modules, and to demonstrate the newly developed capability to receive upgraded software from a remote location. Everything else was off-limits. He glanced at Bergeron, wondering if he had remembered to switch on the system's automatic engagement mode when this round of sea trials began.

The incoming missile streaked across ADAS's thirty-mile buffer, closing the protective gap quickly. At two thousand meters, it was inside the defensive capabilities of everything but the Phalanx Close-In Weapons System. CIWS was a 20 mm Vulcan Gatling-type gun capable of firing 4,500 rounds per minute, which worked out to seventy-five slugs every second. Serving as a last resort, it placed a wall of titanium-tipped rounds between the ship and an incoming threat. As Kreamer watched the screen, the deck gun sprang into action, engaged the missile and blew it out of the sky.

"R2-D2!" Bergeron laughed out loud, glancing over at Kreamer.

The Nautech engineer nodded at the nickname commonly assigned to CIWS due to its distinctive barrel-shaped radome resembling the *Star Wars* droid.

"Didn't know if you had it turned on," he said in an exhale, realizing all at once that he had been holding his breath for the last few seconds of the missile's flight.

"Sure did."

"Hey, I'm up," Kreamer said, pointing to the screen. The new test case was downloading upgraded software from a remote location. "Time to walk you through the download sequence. Go to security, upload, new, operating, overwrite. She'll ask for your PIN when you get there."

Bergeron followed the directions, arriving at a gateway to system security.

"Okay. Verify acceptance," Kreamer said.

"How?"

"Your PIN. The system knows who you are. She's waiting for—"

The ship rolled, interrupting Kreamer. Bergeron's water bottle slipped from its holder on the side of his chair, bounced onto the floor and began rolling away.

"Damn!"

"Hold on," Kreamer said, getting out of his seat to

retrieve the bottle. "She'll wait for you. This is one hell of a storm."

He grabbed Bergeron's water bottle before it could escape farther and hopped back into his chair. "Here you go," he said, handing the plastic bottle back to Bergeron. "Did you enter your PIN already?"

"Not yet."

He stared hard at the screen. "You didn't already enter your PIN?"

"No. What's the matter?"

Kreamer drew back, said, "This isn't right. The simulated download has already started. She should have waited for your PIN."

"Was there a time-out to a default?"

Kreamer blinked a few times and squinched his face into a mass of wrinkles. "There shouldn't have been, but that would explain it. How could there be a default? That would bypass the system's basic security." He glanced at Bergeron, who was shaking his head, indicating the programmer had lost him.

"Once acceptance is validated," Kreamer explained, "the new download acts like an e-mail with a virus attached. It automatically installs, replacing the appropriate sections with the new versions. Security is dependent on the operator accepting the e-mail in the first place with his PIN. Since the operator is already logged into the system, he has authorization to accept. But you didn't give your PIN, so how does she know you're authorized to accept an upgrade?"

"In a real situation, how does the message reach the ship?"

Kreamer was staring at the screen and did not answer. Bergeron was about to repeat his question when the software engineer threw him a glance as if he was awakening from a nap, and said, "Line of sight. Either infrared or microwave. The new software version rides on the carrier beam right into the conning station. That's why you want to have positive validation. I'll write an EDR. Damn! I hate it when this stuff doesn't work," Kreamer said as he gathered information for his engineering design report.

"Is this the first test? At sea, I mean?" Bergeron asked.

"No. We did a mock-up on the *Ike*. I was a ship rider when she sailed through the Straits of Magellan. You think this storm is bad? The one during *Ike*'s trials was unbelievable. Worst I've ever seen. We were tossed around like a cork on a pond. It was awesome."

"The download worked okay then?"

"I think so. Yeah."

Kreamer crossed his arms and settled back in his chair. On screen, the system finished its simulated download and informed them the test was complete. Bergeron touched a few controls, adjusting the monitor's format. Flight operations continued launching F-18s into the stormy night.

"We have the same load as the *Ike*," Kreamer said after a few seconds, referring to the software program loaded into the system at the Nautech lab in San Diego. "The ADAS systems for *Eisenhower* and *Reagan* went through testing within six months of each other. Same production team, same software engineers, same test. We didn't write any EDRs during the *Eisenhower*'s trials. Everything worked perfectly."

Without taking his eyes off the screen, Bergeron asked, "Were you the only rider on the *Ike?*"

"No. There was woman engineer with me. She left the company right after we got back."

"Could she have written an EDR?"

"I'm sure she didn't. Our program manager isn't going to be happy about this. He went to the academy and has a thing about giving sailors systems that work first time every time. He'll want to know why we didn't see this on the *Ike*."

"Were you the one who walked them through the download section?"

"No. The other engineer did. But she would have written it up if the security gate wasn't working properly. I'm sure she didn't. I'm familiar with every EDR that came out of the *Eisenhower*'s trials."

He lapsed into silence, his jaw taking on a hard set as he stared into the distance above Bergeron's console.

"I'm sure of it," Kreamer said almost to himself a good thirty seconds later.

10

Northwest of Sirik, the Iranian coastline concealed thousands of caves and valleys extending all the way around the curving horn of the Strait of Hormuz to Bandar-e-Abbas, then southwest to the city of Bandar-e Lengeh. From the earliest annals of recorded history, travel throughout the region had been known to be treacherous, undertaken only by those who had the means, the confidence and the courage to defend themselves with lethal force.

A stiff wind blowing east from the Persian Gulf gusted intermittently off the water, stirring up a grainy dust that irritated Ali Ansari Hasseim's eyes as he and his party made their way on foot through the mountainous territory between the Govasmand and Guvasmand valleys. Hasseim and four of his most trusted lieutenants were on their way to meet with one of the minor Shiite brotherhoods whose members had merged with his a'mjuur against the invading Americans. It was specifically this small militia that was central to Hasseim's plan. Because of its location, this was where he would store and operate the microwave transmitter that would download new software into the aircraft carrier's defense system. Two of Hasseim's companions carried money for the militia; the other two were outfitted with Stinger missiles. In spite of the terrain, each lieutenant easily carried the thirty-pound air defense weapon strapped across his back.

A night bird sounded a mournful alarm, its cry piercingly shrill in the forsaken wilderness where for the past two hours the only sounds Hasseim and his soldiers had heard were those of their own labored breathing and the measured cadence of their footsteps treading on the beaten dirt trails that wound through the knee-high underbrush.

Hasseim turned and whispered to the man immediately behind him, "Let's rest for a minute. We should be met anytime now."

The four men fanned out away from their commander and peered into the night, good soldiers forever concerned with security.

Hasseim eased his backpack from his shoulders, removed a canteen containing sweet water from the oasis at Garmeh and Khoor, and propped the pack under his haunches for cushioning against the hard ground.

"Ali Ansari Hasseim." He heard his name as a man he recognized from previous meetings emerged from the darkness. "This way."

They followed the guide down a series of steep paths leading to one of the small grottos tucked into the mountainous countryside above the strait. The man leading them pulled a blanket away from the cave's opening, exposing a space lit by kerosene lanterns hanging from hooks driven into the stone walls. Coming in from the windy darkness, the yellow light created an ambiance of welcoming warmth. A group of two dozen men sat on the stone floor, conversing quietly and sipping hot tea from small clay cups.

Roughly half the insurgents were outfitted with modern TAR-21 assault rifles.

The remaining soldiers were armed with a variety of guns. A few carried early-model Uzis. Hasseim noticed some had older Kalashnikov AK-47s, good and reliable under almost any conditions. Among the rifles there were even a couple of vintage .30-caliber M1 Garand carbines. Ammunition diversity was one of the problems every militia in the Middle East faced. Procuring weapons over long periods of time from many different sources produced an inventory requiring numerous caliber ammunition. It was a logistics nightmare.

After introductions were completed, Hasseim stood and spoke.

"The a'mjuur militia welcomes you to fight with us. We've been working with your leaders for more than two months planning a strategy that will strike a significant blow to the American forces occupying our land." He glanced at his watch and said, "Two Black Hawk helicopters are scheduled to fly over this region in less than an hour. As a show of our strength, we will engage them with American-made Stinger missiles."

Hasseim nodded to his companions, and the two missile bearers came forward, each holding a missile in its carrying case. With drilled experience, they swiftly unpacked the man-portable air defense system, laying the weapons onto the cave floor. The men rose and gathered around the weapons, murmuring their approval.

"We wish to demonstrate our capability because we will require your help during the upcoming attack. Below us is the strait's narrowest point. An aircraft carrier sailing through the channel will be less than five miles from shore. That's more than the stated range for a Stinger or a Grail."

He paused and gazed at his audience, receiving assurance that they were still attentive to his words. The men's eyes were fixed on Hasseim with an intensity he found encouraging.

"Before an attack on the carrier will be successful," he continued, "we must transmit a message to disable their electronic shields. This we will do with a microwave machine, and it must be done from this location with your help. We're here tonight to convince you that we have the technology to defeat the Americans. We will show you our power by bringing down two attack helicopters."

In the back of his mind, Hasseim pushed aside the nagging thought that his intel about the Black Hawk's schedule might not be good. He had watched the choppers fly their daily embassy route last week and the week before, and his source in Baghdad told him the flight plan had indeed been filed for this night's trip. But with so much at stake, Hasseim couldn't help but worry. He needed this militia to believe in the a'mjuur's power.

This was the perfect spot from which to download the computer code disabling the ADAS defense system. The program's second half was scheduled to arrive from Paris within days, and the USS *Reagan* would pass through the strait a week later. The window of opportunity was small.

Encouraging their hosts to handle the missile launchers, Hasseim's lieutenants hefted the launch tubes onto one man's and then another's shoulders, agreeing enthusiastically that the weapon was indeed light for the work it could do. When Hasseim said he had access to a few hundred missiles, the militia members were clearly impressed.

"Let's go wait for the Black Hawks," Hasseim said.

The lieutenants perched the missile launchers onto their shoulders and followed Hasseim outside. They moved about four hundred yards apart, each seeking a level spot on solid ground. The men from the militia divided themselves equally between the two, joining them at their positions.

The wait was not long. Through his binoculars, Hasseim could see the two Black Hawk helicopters when they were more than ten miles away. They were flying east over the Persian Gulf, coming his way.

"Get ready," he said loud enough for everyone to hear. "They'll be upon us in a few minutes."

"Ready," the first gunner said, swinging the launcher toward the distant helicopters.

"Ready," the second gunner echoed, duplicating his cohort's motion.

The militiamen sat silently on the ground, watching as the aircraft approached.

"Engaged," the gunners said almost simultaneously as the airships came into range.

"Fire," Hasseim commanded.

The Stingers emitted a sharp pop resembling the discharge from a large-caliber bullet, followed by a whooshing sound that was quickly swallowed by the wind coming off the water. Twin exhaust flames shot from the back end of the launching tubes, illuminating for a few moments the hard faces of the men. The missiles streaked forward, finding their targets within a split second of each other.

The helicopters exploded into spectacular fireballs that drenched the countryside with orange light. The thunderous detonations rocked the hills, coming so close together they echoed through the valleys as one. The choppers' twisted blades continued rotating in slow motion as the airships fell like rocks, straight for the water below. They splashed clumsily into the Gulf, their fuel tanks continuing to burn even as the twisted fuselages sank slowly beneath the surface. The water hissed, bubbled and steamed like a witch's caldron for almost a minute until the battered frames lost all buoyancy and slid downward through the currents to the sandy bottom.

When Hasseim gazed at the men who had witnessed his militia's power, he could see the admiration in their eyes. There was no question they would follow him as he moved forward to strike a much more significant blow against the Americans. Black Hawk helicopters were worthy targets, but compared to an aircraft carrier, they were little more than target practice.

11

Akira Tokaido's fingers moved in a blur as they flew over his keyboard. Due to the nine-hour time difference, it was a little after three o'clock in the afternoon in San Diego when Mack Bolan's Paris locale half a world away crossed over into the next day. At the same time Tokaido was gathering information about electronic defense systems deployed onboard United States aircraft carriers, the Executioner began his midnight assault on McCarthy's Paris warehouse.

True to Kurtzman's prediction, Nautech Corporation had jumped at the opportunity to hire a talented "computer engineer" who was relocating to Southern California from one of the obscure government agencies in Washington, D.C. The fact that he came with a valid security clearance meant the new programmer could immediately be put to work in the software lab where an overload of system faults from the recently deployed USS *Ronald Reagan* was bogging down an entire team of software design engineers.

After receiving a one-hour briefing showing him how to access the list of a few thousand active EDRs, each of which described the specific symptoms of a software glitch requiring corrective action, Tokaido was turned loose to work under the direction of an engineer named Leon Kreamer, who had just returned from a two-month assignment as a ship rider onboard the *Reagan*.

The software and systems test lab where the Stony Man hacker was put to work was more overloaded than it had ever been. A demonstration was being conducted for a Navy fact-finding team dispatched from the Pentagon to investigate the reasons so many faults were being reported from the *Reagan*. From the segments of conversation reaching Tokaido's ears, he could tell the meeting was not going well. One of the senior Navy officers was lambasting Kreamer in a classic display of what it meant to cuss like a sailor. Two other officers joined in, pushing the tirade to a crescendo before it abruptly ended with the visitors storming off to caucus in private. Kreamer, the stress from the meeting evident on his face, paused for a second to take a deep breath, pushed his longish dirty-blond hair away from his eyes and headed for Tokaido's workstation.

"Hey, man, how're you doing?" he asked in a sigh as he flopped into a chair.

Tokaido glanced his way, answering as his fingers continued to type.

"Okay, Leon. HR got me everything I need. Docking station, badge, daytime access into the lab, I'm all set."

"Good." He stared at Tokaido for a few moments, looking vaguely expectant. "Can you hear me okay?"

"Yeah. I always wear them when I program." He grinned, his head bobbing to the beat coming through his earbuds. "Shuts out the outside, you know?"

"Okay," Kreamer said, a thin smirk forming on his face. "Sorry I haven't spent any time getting you onboard. I'm still trying to catch up from my stint on the *Reagan*."

"Good duty?" Tokaido asked.

"Yeah, it is if you like that stuff. The hours are tough, I mean, we're on a 24/7 schedule so your time gets all screwed up, but it's cool seeing the troops actually using the equipment. It also gives you a whole new perspective on why it's important to close EDRs quickly. When you're sitting next to a sailor who can't do something because of a software glitch, you really feel for him. Never mind getting hammered by the brass."

"You were a ship rider on the *Eisenhower,* too, weren't you?" Kreamer gave him a funny look, causing him to quickly add, "One of the other guys here said I probably wouldn't see much of you because you're always gone. He said something about you being out on the *Eisenhower* when she went through her sea trials."

"Oh. Yeah, I was. We had some tough times on the *Ike.*"

"Were you the only ship rider? I mean, does Nautech send more than one? Just curious. From what I hear, only the best engineers get to go."

Kreamer glanced at his watch, absentmindedly and said, "The number varies. Usually it's two or three. There were two of us on the *Ike.* I was the only one on the *Reagan,* but that's because she and the *Ike* went through test and prove-out together. Both systems have the same software load, so the *Reagan* got the benefit of being the second one through. A lot of bugs were already worked out by the time we deployed her."

"Still a lot of EDRs, though," Tokaido said.

"Too many. How're you doing on the ones we gave you?"

"Just about done. Two or three left."

Kreamer's eyebrows shot up.

"When you say done, you mean you've read them and understand the problem?"

"Nope. Fixed them, ran each patch through the simulator and sent them on to the checker."

Kreamer stared hard at the new employee for a few seconds before saying, "Let me get in here and look for a minute."

Tokaido slid his seat away from the desk surface, making room for Kreamer to move in and reach the keyboard.

"Holy shit, man," the engineer said, shaking his head. "This is unbelievable. You've written complete patches? Where'd you learn to write code?"

Tokaido shrugged. "I've taken a ton of courses," he answered as Kreamer continued tabbing from one EDR to the next. "MIT, Stanford, you know. Learned from some wicked talented people."

"Wow." Kreamer restored the work on the screen and pushed himself away from the console. "Nice going. I can't believe it. You're the best programmer I've ever seen."

Tokaido snapped his bubble gum a few times and grinned.

"Can you work some overtime tonight? I don't want you to get burned out, but we really have to make a huge dent in these EDRs. The Navy's all over us because the *Reagan*'s on its way to the Gulf. They want all the faults closed before she gets there."

"Sure."

"Thanks." Kreamer stood and took a few steps before turning back. "I just thought of something. When I was on the *Reagan,* we had a fault I documented with an EDR. I planned on getting back to it, but I'm really overloaded and you can probably do it just as well. Go into the log and sort by author so you can find it. It occurred during the trial that tested download capability. The system acted like it was ready to accept a new software download without verifying the operator's PIN. At the time I wondered why we hadn't seen it on the *Ike* since they both have the same software load. Also, go into the log from the *Ike* and see if maybe the other ship rider wrote something up. I don't think she did, which makes me wonder why we didn't see the glitch if the loads are the same."

"Okay," Tokaido replied. "What's her name so I can sort the *Eisenhower*'s EDRs by author?"

"Marlene Piaseczna," Kreamer replied, spelling out her last name.

Despite his intimate familiarity with the late engineer's name, Tokaido wrote it on the pad next to his console.

"Oh, security," Kreamer said, looking at his watch as he started walking away, suddenly in a hurry. "At the end of your shift, you'll have to leave the lab. Just go to the caf or something for about ten minutes. People with daytime access to the lab don't have it 24/7. Yours is only good to six-fifteen. I'll enter you into the database so in the future you'll be able to stay until midnight, but tonight you'll have to ask Biff to let you back in. Have you met him yet?"

Tokaido shook his head.

"He's the second shift janitor. Long hair, tats, very strange guy. Has a whole story. He'll let you back into the lab after six-thirty. I have to run off to a meeting, but I'll get you on the temp list for tonight with security. Biff should be in any time now, okay?"

Nodding in time to the music blaring through his earbuds, Tokaido responded, "Gotcha."

Kreamer smiled, gave him a thumbs-up and walked away.

Tokaido turned to his screen, pressed a few keys and

jumped to the Nautech Human Resources database he
had hacked into minutes before Kreamer began taking
his tongue-lashing from the visiting Navy personnel. He
scrolled through the employment records, finding
Sherry Krautzer, David Thompson, Wesley Maple and
Marlene Piaseczna. They had all started within six
months of one another, none was married, all under
twenty-five years old. Of the four, only two—
Thompson and Piaseczna—had been assigned to the
ADAS program and granted security clearances to
access the lab.

Tokaido leaned back in his chair, his mind processing the data. He had assumed all four had been on the
ADAS program and held lab clearances. Without it,
how could they have downloaded the amount of code
comprising the operating system in such a short time?
It was definitely more than a two-person job. He wrote
their initials on the pad next to Piaseczna's name,
circling hers and the initials DT to remind himself they
were the only ones with access. He'd get back to that
puzzle later.

Closing the screen, Tokaido jumped to the *Reagan*'s
EDR database. After sorting the entries by author, he
selected the one Kreamer had written and began reading.

12

Despite being sheathed in his wet suit's thermal skin, the Executioner could feel the temperature difference as he slid into the Seine's cool ripples at the Pont au Change. Strapped to his back was a waterproof dive bag containing his combat belt, weapons and night-vision goggles. McCarthy's warehouse was less than half a mile downstream in an isolated section on the triangular tip of Île de la Cité, a short walk on land from the Palais de Justice. It would take Bolan approximately fifteen minutes to swim there.

McCarthy's Family was part of a larger international crime organization. Back at Stony Man Farm, Hal Brognola had shown Bolan classified documents concerning the business activities of the men he was about to encounter. In addition to the expected drug smuggling and burglary, McCarthy's European operations had expanded into white slavery, selling children as young as ten years old into deplorable conditions.

He steered himself toward shore where McCarthy's warehouse could be seen in the distance as a darker rectangle against the inky night sky. A medium-sized tanker, bobbing slightly on the river's surface, was secured to an industrial pier connected by a series of ramps to the warehouse's rear loading docks.

The intel had indicated the arrival of a large consignment from Afghanistan the previous day. The manifest declared the incoming cargo to be handwoven carpets, various hides and pelts, and bales of unprocessed wool, but Kurtzman's team had also found evidence in other databases of financial transactions between McCarthy and Afghan warlords involved in the opium trade. The shipment was both good and bad news for Bolan. If the ship's hold contained illicit drugs, McCarthy's men would be hesitant to call in the Paris authorities when he began his assault. On the other hand, additional security would most certainly be in place until the illegal goods were moved off-site to another location.

The midnight sky was moonless when Bolan's belly scraped the Seine's sandy bottom fifty yards upstream from the tanker. The lighted ends of three cigarettes dancing in the darkness like summer fireflies indicated the presence of guards patrolling the loading ramps. Their casual pace and easy conversation carrying across the shallows to Bolan's ears indicated they were not expecting trouble, but the Executioner suspected he would find them armed, most likely with automatic assault rifles.

Maintaining his low profile, he crawled silently through the sand, using the shadows and shore undulations to mask his approach until he reached the edge of the wide pier and slipped underneath. A trio of river rats was startled by his sudden presence, baring their teeth and hissing their displeasure at his intrusion before scampering away. Pulling himself tight to one of the barnacle-encrusted pilings supporting the pier, Bolan remained silent and still, listening to the activity on the dock above. The men were speaking in French, discussing gambling.

While keeping one ear on their conversation, Bolan loosened the strap holding the dive bag on his back and withdrew the Beretta 93-R. Its suppressor was attached, and the combat veteran knew without checking that the first round was chambered because one of the rules of stealth survival was to always do things the same way. When the air was thick with hot lead, it was better to know without having to check that the ammo pouch on the right contained 9 mm magazines because they were never stored in the left one. Holding the pistol at the ready in one hand, Bolan unzipped and slipped out of his wet suit and pulled on his shoes. He was dressed in black pants and a black long-sleeve shirt that enabled him to blend into the dark shadows.

A familiar sense of power enveloped him when he cinched the combat belt around his waist, checked the hip holster carrying his Desert Eagle, placed his night-vision goggles over his eyes and prepared to spring into action. The critical ingredient was the element of surprise, a factor Bolan knew was in his favor this night.

From the guard's voices, the Executioner figured they were within twenty yards of his position. On the wide-open pier, they would have no place to seek cover. If they were smart, they'd end up tied and gagged while he completed his mission.

With his unsuspecting prey chatting about their weekend plans, Bolan climbed to the pier's uppermost supporting beams so he'd be able to swing his body in one movement onto the dock. As he pulled his legs up under him to provide the explosive force he needed, he thumbed the fire selector on his Beretta to align with three white dots etched into the pistol above its trigger guard. Taking a deep breath, he pushed with his legs, tucked his head and flipped himself head over heels from the crossbeam supporting the decking onto the top surface. He landed in a crouch on his feet, the soles of his shoes slapping the moist wood.

In the eerie green illumination of his night-vision goggles, the Executioner could see that the three men were armed with Heckler & Koch MP-7 personal defense weapons slung across their chests on olive drab canvas slings. The stubby automatic submachine guns fired 4.6 mm rounds from banana clips holding up to forty slugs, and were outfitted with sound suppressors, a detail indicating that the men assigned to guard McCarthy's docks preferred to take care of problems themselves rather than call in law-enforcement agencies. The slings held the weapons a few inches above the guards' belt lines, ready to be grabbed and placed into service in a split second.

"What's that?" one of the men asked as all three turned toward the sound of Bolan's feet hitting the deck. They peered into the thick black night, their hands inching toward the MP-7s.

"Freeze!" Bolan said in a authoritarian voice, training his pistol on the trio.

The man closest reached for his weapon, his hands moving in a blur, apparently intending to find the trigger with his right hand while swinging the blazing barrel outward with his left, spraying a lethal stream of lead into the intruder. The man's finger was successful in finding the trigger, but an instant before he could squeeze off the first round, Bolan's 93-R coughed three times in rapid succession.

Ambient noise on the dock completely swallowed the pistol's sound, as the Beretta's 9 mm Parabellum rounds drilled three neat holes in the would-be gunner's forehead, toppling him straight back like a felled tree. His head bounced slightly upon impact with the wood, his limp hand sliding away from the weapon on his chest as his corpse came to rest.

The dead man's partners were trained to react, and they did so by grasping frantically for their machine guns, attempting the same maneuver the first man had just proved to be unsuccessful. With their full attention focused on bringing their weapons to bear, neither thought to dive onto the deck to reduce their silhouette and create distance between themselves.

Seeing their reaction, the Executioner threw himself horizontally to the right, pulling the trigger on his 93-R as he flew through the air three feet above the pier's wooden surface. One of the guards was successful loosing a stream of lead on full-auto, slicing the air with 4.6 mm slugs where Bolan had been standing a second earlier. A second burst from the 93-R answered the guard's barrage, hitting him midchest. As the force of the bullets pushed him back, the man's arms pinwheeled, blood surging from his wounds. He ran out of dock surface at about the same time his heart ran out of blood, his lifeless body falling off the side of the pier into the soft sand six feet below.

When Bolan's muscular frame hit the deck, he went into an immediate roll, coming up with the Beretta continuing to spit death in heel-to-toe volleys comprised of three bullets. The final guard was hosing down the area between them, spraying the twenty yards of dock space with hot lead that chewed into the wooden surface, throwing splinters the size of pencils in all directions. His aim was low because he was attempting to run toward the warehouse while firing, making the MP-7's recoil on full-auto hard to control. Before he was able to direct the automatic fire into his adversary, one of Bolan's rounds struck him in the thigh, spinning him sideways. A millisecond later, another slug struck him in the side of the face, the bullet's force acting in concert with his own backward momentum to lift him off his feet. As he flew through the air, his finger froze in a death grip on the MP-7's trigger, peppering a long volley of muffled bullets randomly into the sky. The man was dead before he landed, his body sliding a few feet after impact before settling into a grotesque pose with his left arm twisted awkwardly behind his back.

Bolan sprinted to a spot behind a creosote-coated piling and dropped to one knee. While gazing back and forth across the dock for new threats, he ejected the magazine from his Beretta, reached into an ammunition pouch for a fresh one and rammed it home into the pistol's ammo port. He believed the sounds of the river and the city beyond had probably been adequate to completely cover the sounds of the brief firefight, but he wanted to make sure there were no reinforcements on the way. There was a good chance no one inside had heard the automatic fire, as his enemies' weapons had been outfitted with silencers and the suppressed muzzles had been pointing away from the warehouse. The exchange had also been quick, but Bolan had not survived for years on hellfire trails around the globe by taking unnecessary risks. He remained behind the thick wooden post until he was convinced no one was being dispatched. When he was ready to move on, he wiped away the sweat on his forehead and drew the Desert Eagle. With loaded weapons in both hands, the Executioner began his approach to find the late Michael McCarthy's big bodyguard who would give him information about where the computer code protecting American aircraft carriers was being sent.

The night was very dark, enabling Bolan in his black clothing to approach the back side of the warehouse invisibly without being seen. As he moved quickly from the pier to the side of the building, he touch-checked his gear with the hand holding the Beretta, running experienced fingers over the percussion and smoke grenades, the extra magazines in his ammo pouches loaded and waiting to be called into action.

Ramps from the pier converged onto a concrete staging and loading platform. The concrete area was under the cover of a tin roof extending slightly more than twenty feet from the side of the building. Next to a sliding door, which when opened would create a doorway wide enough to accept crates the size of a small car, a huge propane-powered forklift capable of carrying forty thousand–pound sea containers into the receiving area was plugged into an oversized battery charger. Immediately adjacent to the charger, half a dozen six-foot cylinders of propane stood in a straight row, looking like soldiers at inspection.

Moving silently, Bolan sprinted around the corner of the building, where a wood-framed window with a single pane of glass was set at chest level. The Executioner crept to the edge, and staying low, peered inside.

The night-vision goggles amplified the inside light, creating a detailed scene illuminated as if it was noontime. The warehouse shipping and receiving area was a wide-open room with wooden crates scattered in seemingly random groups throughout. Directly inside the sliding door opening onto the loading dock, a prefabricated office jutted out from the brick warehouse wall. Most of the office wall space on the three nonbrick sides was glass, allowing a supervisor during work hours to watch both the shippers on the dock and the packagers inside. Fewer than one-quarter of the track lights suspended from the thirty-foot ceiling were in use, casting entire sections of the warehouse in dark shadow. Immediately inside the window from Bolan, wooden crates stacked anywhere from three- to ten-feet high stood in various states of assembly.

Four men sitting at a small table outside the office smoked as they played team cribbage, the smoke from their cigarettes hanging in a hazy cloud a few feet above their heads. While Bolan watched, two erupted into complaints while a third moved his scoring peg in a grandiose movement down the board. Propped against the table, within easy reach of the players, were four MP-7s identical to the ones carried by the men guarding the dock.

A voice called out to the card players, and Bolan squeezed his face against the far side of the window frame in order to see that the speaker was Johnny Kohotina. The muscular bodyguard was coming from within the warehouse, drinking a can of beer. The sixteen-ounce cylinder looked comically small in his massive hand as he chugged for a few seconds, lowered the can and let loose a loud belch that could be heard through the windowpane. Across the front of his chest he wore a shoulder holster containing a .40-caliber Glock, the same type of weapon the ex-con had directed at him when he was requesting McCarthy's cooperation at the gangster's body repair shop in Las Vegas.

When he walked by the table on his way into the supervisor's office, Kohotina said something that made the men laugh. Bolan watched the bodyguard enter the glass-walled office and toss his empty beer can into the corner where there had to have been a wastebasket. A few steps away, he opened a refrigerator for another, popped the tab and quickly brought the can to his lips to slurp the bubbling foam. Beer in hand, he left the office and leaned against the wall to watch the cribbage game.

Bolan left the window, hugging the building as he rounded the corner moving back onto the loading dock where he holstered his Beretta. From one of the pouches on his combat belt he withdrew an MK3A2 concussion grenade and two AN-M8 smoke canisters. Leaning against the corner of the warehouse, he set the fuse on the percussion grenade for thirty seconds, pulled the safety pin and rolled the elliptical-shaped bomb across the concrete area toward the propane tanks. It clanged into them as it impacted, coming to rest in the seam between the third and fourth cylinder. With roughly twenty seconds remaining before detonation, Bolan hustled around the corner to the window, pulling the safety pins from the smoke canisters he held in his left hand. He set his night-vision goggles to infrared mode before drawing the Desert Eagle from its hip holster.

Seconds before the percussion grenade exploded, the Executioner opened fire on the window with the Desert Eagle. The hefty .44-caliber slugs blew the wood frame to smithereens, sending a hail of glass shards and wood splinters into the room. The barrage produced the effect Bolan was looking for as the men dived for cover, intent on getting to their submachine guns. Bolan registered the men's trajectories and, like a baseball player at the plate watching a fastball's spin, anticipated their speed and future position. With the Desert Eagle's throaty roar echoing in his ears, Bolan tossed the smoke canisters he was holding in his left hand through the space where the window had been, following in close order with a dive that landed him in a covered position behind two wooden crates.

The percussion grenade on the loading dock detonated, bringing the propane tanks immediately to their flash point. Simultaneous with a shock wave that blew the outside wall into the room, the gas exploded with an eardrum-pulsing force that shook the warehouse. Billowing white smoke pouring from the canisters reduced vision to inches as the air filled with the sound of 4.6 mm rounds being fired on full-auto. It was a panic response, because the gunmen didn't know where or how many enemies they were facing, but the rounds kept the Executioner pinned low behind wooden crates.

As he drew his Beretta, Bolan detected a pattern. His adversaries were sweeping their weapons methodically around the room, the regularity of their firing giving him a window of opportunity almost as predictable as that of a prison spotlight. Replacing the magazine in his Desert Eagle with a fresh one, he waited for the rounds to come his way. On the other side of the crate he was crouching behind, Bolan could hear the slugs ripping through wood, whining and sparking when they hit a nail. Wood smoke mingling with the smoke canister's chemical outpouring produced an acrid combination that stung his eyes. When the volley from the gunmen passed his spot, he peered around the corner of the shipping container, zeroing in on the muzzle-flashes winking in the thick smoke.

Springing to his feet, the Executioner squeezed off four triplets so close together the Beretta's silenced sputtering sounded like a zip gun. A medley of angry howls and shrieks of fury told him he had been successful finding his targets. He crawled away from his position, putting space between his last spot of fire. There were reinforcements arriving from within the warehouse, their presence marked with an increase in the firing volume that quickly reached an insane crescendo. A section of the warehouse adjacent to where the propane tanks had exploded caught fire, setting off the automatic sprinklers. The sound of fire alarms and water being sprayed from the ceiling added to the racket, turning the scene into utter chaos. Then, all at once, the firing stopped.

"Hey! Hey!" a deep voice called out in the sudden silence that made Bolan realize his ears were ringing. "What the hell is this? What's going down here?"

Keeping low, Bolan shouted, "We want Kohotina! Out on the dock with your hands above your head!"

There was a pause of about ten seconds before the Executioner's words were met with an intense flurry of lead, indicating the security force was a well-trained unit. Kohotina's attempt to negotiate was a ploy, intended to get everyone into position before running a play. From the muzzle-blasts and the infrared outlines visible through the smoke, Bolan realized they had zeroed in on his section of the room. Two teams of three gunmen each were moving in from both sides, attempting to squeeze him in a pinchers maneuver.

Moving swiftly between two stacks of reinforced crates, Bolan fired 3-round bursts from the Beretta, weaving the pistol's autofire stutter around the authoritarian single shots flaming from his Desert Eagle. A mad volley of steady fire sliced through the air in a floor-to-ceiling arc as one of the Desert Eagle's powerful bullets hit home, apparently shoving the victim backward as his finger froze on his MP-7's trigger. The submachine gun's bolt finally clicked open on a empty chamber at the same instant Bolan let loose with a salvo of .44 Magnum slugs aimed directly into the muzzle-blasts of the three gunmen circling his position from the right.

One by one, as neatly as in a shooting gallery, the hazy forms of his enemies were cast to the side by the forceful bullets from the Desert Eagle. Moans from the wounded provided an increasingly loud countermelody to the percussive automatic fire that filled his ears, telling him he was turning the tide of the battle.

The pace of the firefight suddenly stepped up in a final all-out assault by the warehouse crew, with the result that lead was flying through the air close enough for the skin on Bolan's face to feel their hot breath as he darted behind cover. Although the smoke was beginning to dissipate, his infrared goggles continued to give him a competitive advantage as he watched his enemies' silhouettes dash from one crate to the next. With the patience of a cat sitting outside a mouse hole, he waited until the men slipped into his fire lanes. The Beretta and Desert Eagle sang a swift duet of death as Bolan picked off the scampering gunmen, finally impressing upon the survivors that the intruders possessed a sight advantage. There was urgent shouting back and forth for a few seconds before all became quiet.

"Hey!" Kohotina's voice boomed through the hazy air. "What's the deal?"

"Same as in Vegas!" Bolan shouted.

There was a long pause while Kohotina put the pieces together. "You the one killed the boss?"

"No one had to die. You don't have to, either, Kohotina. Decide now to talk and live, or you can join McCarthy in the grave."

With the bodies of close to a dozen guards scattered around the office cubicle like limp rag dolls, Kohotina was viewing the situation from a dismal perspective. He had no idea how many storm troopers he was facing, but the fact that they were attacking with smoke and percussion grenades was enough to convince him his troops were outclassed.

"Okay!" the big bodyguard shouted, tossing his pistol toward the shattered office. The weapon clattered across the concrete floor for a few feet before hitting a piece of debris and coming to a spinning stop. Bolan edged toward the expanded window opening he had come in through, keeping the protective cover of the half-assembled shipping crates between himself and his enemies. He didn't know how many men were still inside the warehouse, and wanted to conclude his interview with Kohotina as quickly as possible.

"Out on the dock! Hands above your head!" Bolan shouted before slipping through the window opening. From the outside corner of the building, he watched Kohotina walk onto the loading dock. Keeping himself in the shadows, Bolan began inching away from the burning warehouse, both handguns held at the ready.

"Right there! On your knees! Don't let your hands come down."

The bodyguard did as he was told while Bolan continued moving toward the pier where he could set himself up for his exit. Through his goggles he could see that Kohotina was gazing back and forth along the pier, still unsure how many attackers he was facing.

From behind one of the thick creosote-coated pilings, Bolan called out, "Do you have the computer code?"

"It's gone. Mailed it to a forwarding address."

"What was the name?"

"Piaseczna," Kohotina shouted back, apparently deciding that it was in his interest to tell the truth. "Marlene Piaseczna."

"Where is she now?"

"Her customer hired us to terminate their contract."

"Who's the customer?" Bolan asked, half expecting his prisoner might not know.

"Guy named Hasseim. Ali Ansari Hasseim."

Bolan recognized it was the same name Huntington Wethers had come upon in his research.

Kohotina continued, "He sent us money, I got the code, terminated his contract with the girl and sent his package to a mailbox on the other side of Paris. End of story."

"How'd you find out his name?"

Kohotina, glaring into the darkness, said, "Don't think we won't know your names, too, by next week. You're all dead men."

Behind Kohotina, Bolan could see half a dozen armed guards inside the warehouse waiting to react if the opportunity presented itself. He began moving away from the piling toward the water, dashing from one post to another.

"Stay right where you are until we're gone," he said while increasing the space between himself and the warehouse. "Move too soon, and we'll drop you. Keep 'em up!" It was a tactic that would keep his enemies grounded for about five minutes, giving him time to get away.

When he reached the river's sandy bank, Bolan turned toward the busy section of the island. He moved quickly and surely, reaching a thin stand of trees where he relieved himself of his weapons and combat gear, covering them with his black long-sleeve shirt that he'd peeled off to reveal a multicolored short-sleeve shirt underneath. Before departing, he pulled a signal beacon from one of the web belt's pouches, activated it and buried it in the middle of his cache, knowing Brognola's men would be by to collect the hardware within an hour.

Finger-combing his hair, he walked swiftly away from the sparse woods, crossing a small grassy park before merging with groups of tourists who had come over to Île de la Cité to see the sights at night. Within minutes, he had blended into the pedestrian traffic. By the time McCarthy's men summoned the courage to begin searching for the intruder, Mack Bolan was on his way to the airport.

The team from Stony Man Farm had been too late to stop the transfer from taking place. Computer code capable of disabling an aircraft carrier's defense system was on its way to a terrorist group, but at least Bolan had verified a name. From his shirt pocket he pulled his cell phone and speed-dialed one of Hal Brognola's protected lines.

"Yes, Striker," the big Fed answered.

"Ali Ansari Hasseim. Hunt had his name."

"Yeah, he did. He's the customer?"

"Roger. We missed the mail."

"Go see Akira."

"Wilco. On my way."

Bolan closed his cell phone, put it back in his pocket and reviewed his progress.

They knew who they were looking for, but the Middle East was a huge place. Kurtzman's team at Stony Man Farm was cranking through mountains of data 24/7 trying to find a reference, but locating an autonomous group of terrorists in the regions bordering the Persian Gulf was as good a real-life example of the proverbial needle in a haystack as Bolan could think of.

Although he had been against Akira Tokaido going undercover into Nautech's San Diego plant, Bolan now hoped the hacker had learned something that might narrow their search. Depending on how many drops the terrorist network was using, the computer code may have already reached Hasseim, who would be frantically working to bring the remaining pieces of his strategy together. Bolan's mission was to find the terrorist group before it was able to deal a serious blow to the United States Navy.

13

"I know how they plan to load the new software," Akira Tokaido said as he and Bolan sat on the sidewalk patio of a San Diego restaurant.

Bolan raised his palm to alert the hacker that a waitress was coming up behind him. Not until after she had taken their drink orders and left to fill them did the young man continue as if there had been no interruption.

"Piaseczna's crew got into the lab at night and rewrote a segment of the operating system telling it to accept certain types of software downloads without going through the normal verification process. The disabling code they sold to the terrorists will most certainly be accepted by both the *Ike* and the *Reagan*."

He paused and snapped his gum a few times before adding, "Piaseczna was a ship rider on the *Ike*, where she watched the trapdoor operate. The system should have failed part of its sea trial, but Piaseczna never wrote an EDR documenting the same fault that Kreamer witnessed on the *Reagan*."

"If we know the trapdoor is there, can't the engineers write a software program to prevent it from being used?" Bolan asked.

"Not that easy," Tokaido replied before stopping

short as the waitress reappeared, coming their way with drinks on a silver tray.

She placed the glasses before them and stood back, giving the two men an expectant look.

"We need more time," Bolan said.

The young woman smiled and began edging away. "Call me when you're ready," she said. "No rush."

"Hal contacted the *Reagan* about the problem," Tokaido went on when she was far enough away so he wouldn't be heard, "and Nautech is flying a team of software engineers to rendezvous with her and the *Ike* in the Gulf, but the odds are not good."

Bolan raised his eyebrows over the rim of his tonic water.

"Millions of lines of code," Tokaido explained while shaking his head. "Any one of them could have been edited to turn it into a trapdoor. They have to go through every line, all the way down to the level where's there nothing but ones and zeros."

"Can't the software guys go in and see when the program was changed? The system doesn't automatically keep a record of that?" Bolan asked.

"Good thought, but no. First off, Piaseczna would have made sure they all covered their tracks. Remember, these are engineers who wrote the code telling systems to do things like keep track of unauthorized entry. They're the very people who could easily evade security. Secondly, even if they missed erasing all the evidence, their activity would get lost among the thousands of changes that have rippled through the software ever since factory test back in San Diego. Actually, it's part of the sea trial process to keep the software in flux so glitches that show up can be fixed. Considering the effect of each change on linked programs, the system would say there have been tens of thousands of changes. No way a team can efficiently sift through all those transactions looking for a trapdoor that might not even be visible. But it's the only course of action available right now."

Jumping ahead, Bolan asked, "You said you know how they're going to do it."

Tokaido nodded. "The system is designed to take downloads in a few different ways, one of them being by microwave." He glanced at Bolan and said, "Yeah, the microwave machine you captured up in Manitoba. At first I thought they built it just to show they were good engineers, but now I think it was part of the solution they delivered. I'll bet the terrorists have another microwave transmitter just like the one you found. They'll download the instructions to drop the shields directly into the line of code edited by Piaseczna."

"Will the ship know?"

"When the first missile hits the flight deck without advance warning, they'll know something is wrong. The crew will react and go into emergency mode, but there's no telling how long it will take to get the system back in sync. A few hundred Stingers could damage a carrier to the point of no return, causing so many secondary explosions it would be impossible to bring her back. A watery version of a downward spiral."

They fell into silence, each pondering a mental image of Stinger missiles raining unabated onto a carrier.

"There's more news," Tokaido said after the brief pause.

"What is it?" Bolan asked.

"The Nautech janitor who lets me into the lab at night. I think he's the fifth member, the partner Robbie Maxwell suspected but could never find. I think Biff was working with Piaseczna."

"Why?" Bolan asked.

"Because her four partners didn't all have the access to the lab they needed to alter the operating system and generate new code. Only two did. Biff could have let them in the same way he does me. He asked why I wrote Piaseczna's name on my desk pad. I also had the initials of the others, which he would have recognized."

"What did you tell him?"

"That Kreamer told me to look up some EDRs they wrote. But I don't think he believed me. Someone went through my desk last night. He got me suspicious, so I checked him out. It took some digging, but sure enough, he has five hundred grand in a Cayman account."

IT WAS ONE O'CLOCK in the morning when Bolan burst from the hallway into Randall Casperian's tiny bedroom, interrupting the janitor's hurried packing. His flying tackle propelled them both away from the bed where the man had been throwing clothes into an open suitcase. They landed on the worn carpet a good five feet away from the suitcase, out of reach should a weapon be among the items being packed.

"Hello, Biff," Bolan said through clenched teeth as he pinned his victim to the floor. "Are you going somewhere?"

The man struggled under the weight of his attacker.

Bolan pushed himself off the man and took a few steps back.

"On you knees, lock your hands behind your head," he said as he aimed his Beretta at the man.

The janitor did as he was told, glaring and cursing. "What do you want?" he asked sullenly.

"Information," Bolan replied. "You answer my questions well enough, you get to live. Bad answers, I blow your brains out. Really bad answers, I start shooting you in other places. You ready?"

Biff glared at him with eyes full of hate. His breathing was labored, and he was swaying slightly.

"Who was the customer?" Bolan asked.

Biff remained silent for a moment. "Don't know. That wasn't part of my deal. All I did was get them into the lab."

"Half a mil is pretty good pay for just being a doorman."

The janitor looked up, fixing Bolan with his eyes. "How do you know about that?"

As a reply, the Executioner slid the Beretta's barrel to the rear and let it fly forward, manually chambering a round. Leveling the pistol at the man's forehead, he said, "Not a good answer, Biff."

"No! Wait! I'm telling you I don't know. She never told me details. All they wanted me to do was get them into the lab at night. The code was going to someone in one of those Iran or Iraq places. She made a trip over there last December for a test. That's all I know."

"Sullivan!" Bolan shouted while flicking the pistol's safety on and sliding it back into its holster.

Three men wearing FBI field jackets ran into the room. They went directly to Biff and began securing his hands behind his back with nylon wrist ties while one of them read his Miranda rights in an authoritarian monotone. With a final glance over his shoulder, Bolan slipped out the apartment to a sedan waiting at the curb to take him to the airport where he was booked on a flight to Washington, D.C.

Time was running short.

"HOW IRONIC," Aaron Kurtzman said from his end of the conference table, "that an attack on American aircraft carriers might be executed with missiles designed and manufactured in the United States." Looking in Tokaido's direction, he added, "Surely, with the ships being aware of the threat, our technology can prevent such an event from occurring."

"Not so," Tokaido responded. "The *Reagan* is due to enter the Gulf within a week, spending a few days on a top secret mission in the narrow channels around the Strait of Hormuz. Even knowing ADAS might be compromised, what are her choices?"

He paused for a few moments to move the wad of bubble gum he was chewing to the other side of his mouth before saying, "We don't know when or from where the instructions to drop the electronic shields will come, so the ship is faced with either giving up her mission until new code is written, which would take upward of a year, or going into harm's way with full knowledge she may be vulnerable to attack. There's not much the crew can do."

"All over money. These engineers sold out their country for a few million dollars. And look what it got them," Bárbara Price said.

"It was more than that," Brognola stated. "Piaseczna had problems adjusting to the culture at Nautech. She may or may not have gone in with a chip on her shoulder, but once she got there, she couldn't cope in an industry dominated by white males. We've done in-depth background checks on her and the other four. They were all misfits. Sad people waiting for a chance to get back at a company they believed mistreated them by not respecting their intelligence."

"Not too different from kids who shoot up their high schools," Carmen Delahunt said.

In a tone uncharacteristically laced with pessimism, Price said, "None of that matters now." She grabbed a remote from the center of the conference table and pointed it at the far wall. As a projection screen descended from the ceiling, she asked, "Akira, is the feed from the drones real-time?"

"It is," he answered, "but that's not what matters. The data is real-time, but the value comes from analysis." He gazed around the room and said, "We have reason to believe the new instructions will be relayed to the *Reagan* via microwave. That's why they had the transmitter Striker captured in Manitoba. At first I thought it was an exotic weapon meant to demonstrate their engineering skills, but after working on the systems in San Diego, I'm convinced the microwave generator was designed to be their downloading mechanism."

"How exactly does it work?" Brognola asked.

"Line of sight. Load a flash drive containing the code into a laptop, connect it to the transmitter, and send the new instructions riding on a microwave right into the aircraft carrier's conning tower. Thanks to Piaseczna and her cohorts, the ship's system is open and waiting to receive the message."

"But as you say," Delahunt pointed out, "Striker captured their transmitter."

"We believe Hasseim's group has another one." Kurtzman jumped ahead to the conclusion before Tokaido could answer. "Remember we said it was a low-tech product? Not state-of-the-art at all. Something they could easily reproduce."

Tokaido spit his gum into a wrapper and tossed it into the wastebasket in the corner.

"Exactly," he agreed. "We learned Piaseczna made a trip to the Gulf last December. U.S. drones have that entire area under constant surveillance. They listen and record everything, even when they're not looking for anything specific. I wrote a program to search the tapes from December for microwave signatures. If Piaseczna was there for a demonstration, they'd probably fire up the transmitter."

Price pushed a button on the remote, and a topographical chart of the Persian Gulf came onto the screen. The map was covered with superimposed images and symbols.

"We've used satellite tracking many times to find individual ships. This is similar, except we're looking for specific frequencies in the tapes. Track the signal back to the drone that recorded it, and we get a general area of where a microwave transmission occurred," Tokaido said.

"And that's them? It's that simple?" Brognola asked.

"No. Microwave transmissions come from many sources. Even with statistical analysis applied to this data, all we have is a hunch. A well-informed hunch, but not a slam dunk." He reached forward to take a laser pointer off the table, using it to direct a red beam to an area on the map. "Somewhere around Bandar-e Abbas, in the hills here above the Strait of Hormuz, is where we should be looking."

"What's the terrain there?" Brognola asked, his eyes glued to the screen.

Price pressed a button on the remote, and a satellite photo replaced the topographical map.

Mack Bolan got up out of his chair and walked to the image. "Forests," he said, studying the picture.

"And caves you can't see from the air," Wethers added. "It's not going to be easy finding people holed up in that region. That's for sure."

Kurtzman took a long slug of his coffee and asked, "Can we delay the *Reagan*'s arrival?"

"No," Brognola said with such finality that all at the

table knew immediately he was privy to the ship's top secret mission. "Striker has to stop them from transmitting the code to the ship." Fixing the Executioner with a steely gaze, he added, "You have four days."

Price flipped through her notes and said, "Here's the plan. Striker HELOs into the area, finds Hasseim's militia and takes out the transmitter before they can use it." She glanced down at the paper before her. "The 82nd Airborne has a full brigade waiting to be called in, and the *Reagan's* flight wing is available for air support." She looked up from her notes at Bolan and said, "But you have to destroy the transmitter before they can use it."

The soldier was squinting at the screen as if his eyes could penetrate the forest's canopy. When he spoke, it was with the voice of a seasoned professional weighing battlefield odds. "How many men in the militia?"

"Less than a thousand, and intelligence reports gathered on the ground indicate they're split into at least ten units," Wethers answered.

"Weapons?"

"We have a brief for you," Brognola said before Wethers could respond. "They'll be armed with a collection of old and new guns from all over the world. No rhyme or reason to the hardware, it will be a wide assortment of weapons various warlords were able to obtain over the past fifty years."

"Old or new doesn't matter as long as the weapons can still kill." Price stated the obvious in a soft voice.

"Are we sure we know where the transmitter is?" Bolan asked.

"No," Tokaido spoke up. "Based on satellite and drone data, plus intelligence the CIA assembled on the ground, three locations are probable. Greater than eighty percent probability the transmitter is in one of these three places."

"Eighty percent," Bolan repeated. "Okay."

"Do you want help? Able Team could be made available," Price said.

He hesitated a long moment before answering.

"A brigade from Airborne should be enough. I'll call them in as soon as I find the transmitter. That way if I fail, they'll come in right behind to finish the job."

Silence hung like a blanket over the group while they pondered the implications of the statement.

"Four days before the *Reagan* reaches the Gulf," Brognola repeated. "Let's get to it."

14

A western wind blowing across the water and up the side of the forested hill gave life to dusty whirlwinds that danced for a few seconds between the trees before collapsing to the ground. Ali Ansari Hasseim adjusted his kaffiyeh, tugging it so it covered the crooked scar that ran the length of his left cheek. But it wasn't for the sake of appearances that he repositioned his scarf. The warm wind coming off the Gulf stirred a dry coarse grit into the air, and breathing through the cotton cloth prevented the militant's nostrils and throat from getting irritated.

Gazing down at the Strait of Hormuz hundreds of feet below his position, Hasseim turned the plan of attack over in his mind for what seemed to be the thousandth time. In a concealed cave behind him sat a microwave transmitter, protected from the elements by a camouflaged canvas tarp. Two laptops, a primary and backup unit, were stored with the transmitter, awaiting the computer program that would render the American's aircraft carrier vulnerable. Hasseim and Abbas, his trusted deputy, were the only two who possessed flash drives holding the code. One of them would be present when the deed was done.

He squinted against the glare reflecting off the Gulf's

surface, visualizing the impending attack. His well-developed spy network told him the USS *Ronald Reagan*, the American Navy's newest aircraft carrier, was scheduled to arrive at the strait within days to relieve the *Eisenhower*. He'd receive plenty of updates before the warship actually showed up; knowing when to have everyone in place was not an issue. Precise timing, however, was.

Hasseim was unsure if once the electronic shields dropped, they could be brought back up. He surmised they probably could, which meant there would be a fleeting window of opportunity during which time his forces would have to engage the vessel with their entire arsenal. How he could have neglected to ask the engineer so fundamental a question puzzled him. To overlook such a detail, he must have been preoccupied with ensuring he'd have a sufficient missile inventory, and with coordinating the transactions enabling him to obtain the code. He mentally chastised himself yet again for prematurely ordering the harlot engineer's death. Even after she disrespected him by involving the men from Las Vegas to perform the final transaction, he should have waited. In retrospect, he realized he could have kidnapped the woman and brought her here as an adviser to make sure everything worked properly. There would have been plenty of time to kill her afterward.

The screech of a red-tailed hawk drew his eyes skyward where a pair of the predatory birds soared on thermal updrafts. He shifted his gaze to the distant horizon. Against the haze out past Qeshm Island, he could barely make out the silhouette of an Iranian battleship. Someday, he thought, the imperialist nations would be driven from the region, and the only ships patrolling the Persian Gulf would be from the surrounding nations. Ali Ansari Hasseim stood ready to give his life to make that vision a reality.

The sound of footsteps behind him broke his reverie, and he turned to see Abbas walking quickly toward him.

"Are they ready in Sirik?" Hasseim asked when his subordinate drew close.

"They are. Fifty men with one hundred missiles."

"American Stingers."

"Yes. The other hundred are divided between here and Al Khasab. We'll supplement those with the Grails we have. You look worried."

Hasseim shook his head and replied, "Not worried, concerned. Communication will be critical. Our fighters must understand that once the shields come down, they'll have a limited time to fire their missiles. Let's make sure we have backup plans in place so they'll know the exact instant when we send the code to the ship."

"As soon as we do, we'll engage the target with our missiles. The men in Sirik and Al Khasab will follow our lead and engage the target as soon as we do," Abbas said.

Hasseim nodded, but the way his eyes stared into the distance belied his confidence.

"We will succeed," Abbas said assuredly. "It's our destiny. Fate put the missiles into our hands, fate brought the woman engineer to us and fate will deliver our enemies."

Hasseim remained silent.

"We will succeed," Abbas repeated.

TIMOTHY BERGERON LEANED BACK in his chair and extended his laced fingers to the front, stretching his arms to their full length. His watch was close to ending, closing the log on another uneventful six hours.

Bergeron was thankful for the inactivity. There were

Nautech engineers onboard, and Captain Gifford had briefed the commo and weapons teams concerning a possible virus targeting ADAS. Bergeron didn't like to think what the consequences would be if the system went down. As part of the crew's training, they had watched a film about the USS *Stark,* the frigate that was attacked in 1987 by an Iraqi Mirage F1 fighter jet. ADAS hadn't existed back then, and two Exocet antiship missiles slammed into the *Stark,* killing thirty-seven sailors and wounding twenty-one more. The fact that no weapons had been fired in defense led the Navy to develop ADAS as an automatic means to protect ships. If that went down, everyone and everything onboard would be in grave danger.

The door to the command center opened, and Jim Haley, Bergeron's replacement, entered. He paused for a moment, presumably allowing his eyes to adjust to the dim crimson glow illuminating the room.

"How you doing?" he asked Bergeron, disregarding the official words they were supposed to relate when changing watch.

"No activity," Bergeron replied. "You ready now?"

"Yeah. Consider yourself officially relieved."

Haley climbed into the elevated chair vacated by Bergeron and signed in to the system. Bergeron waited for his replacement to be electronically accepted before signing himself out.

"What do you think about that virus thing?" Haley asked as he progressed through a series of steps checking the system's functionality.

"Man, I don't know. But the Nautech engineers can probably fix anything that happens, so even if there is a virus I don't know if anything bad will happen."

"Remember the *Stark,*" Haley said, as if the words

were a war slogan like "Remember the Alamo" or "Remember the *Maine*."

"I know. With all the planes on deck, not to mention people who might get killed if there was an attack, losing ADAS even for a little while would be a bad news situation."

"Okay. I'm in and the system is operational. Have a good night."

Bergeron gave his shipmate a mock salute, picked up his backpack containing some reading materials and snacks, and left the command center.

Outside the claustrophobic room, the air smelled clean and fresh. The sea was calm, and the nuclear-powered vessel was cruising smoothly toward her destination. She was approximately three days away from the Persian Gulf.

15

The small helicopter circled while Bolan adjusted the Global Positioning System sensor Tokaido had given him back at Stony Man Farm. Based on the data collected from satellites and twice as many Air Force drones as normal that were deployed to cover the region, Kurtzman's cybernetics team had zeroed in on an area they believed sheltered Hasseim's a'mjuur militia. Ten thousand feet below, a forest of ancient cypress and hemlock stretched for a square mile over the hills above the Strait of Hormuz. Kurtzman's group had uplinked the position with the Agency's GPS satellite, enabling Bolan to locate and jump directly into the spot.

Dressed in jungle fatigues, the high points on his face and hands subdued with an irregular pattern of green, brown and black face camouflage, Bolan was all but invisible in the backseat of the two-person high-performance chopper. He and the pilot communicated through wireless earplugs and throat mikes they wore under their oxygen masks.

"Got it," Bolan said, watching the sensor's display.

"Roger." The pilot held the aircraft in a hover while his rider prepared to jump.

Bolan was a tight squeeze for the chopper's passenger seat. He was a large man to begin with, and when he was outfitted with a fully stocked combat belt and weapons, his girth was formidable. The backseat was tapered along the fuselage, shrinking it further. Rather than fight the space, Bolan stood for their short flight from the deck of a Navy frigate stationed below at the Strait of Hormuz awaiting a rendezvous with the USS *Ronald Reagan.*

The pilot's voice came over the intercom. "I'll be right here if you need me. I can drop ten in under thirty."

Bolan was carrying a full battle load. The pouches on his web belt bulged with ammunition and explosives, and his left breast pocket contained a sealed plastic bag filled with water and one magazine containing six orvilles. With a final glance at the GPS sensor, he pulled his night-vision goggles over his eyes, removed his oxygen mask and jumped from the helicopter.

He held his breath as he flew through the atmosphere, quickly reaching terminal velocity with its odd floating sensation. When the small LED altimeter on his parachute's harness told him he was under seven thousand feet, he exhaled and began breathing normally.

"Under seven," he said.

"Roger," the pilot responded. "I see you."

Bolan had executed countless HELO jumps into both hot and cold zones. The pilot would remain at ten thousand feet, comfortably above detection while Bolan free fell through the enemy's coverage, opening his chute when he was too low to be picked up by radar. They were operating in Iranian airspace, and although there was no overt collusion between Iran and the militia they were targeting, you never knew who was helping whom behind the scenes. A HELO entry would allow Bolan to attack his first objective with the element of surprise. After that, he'd have the pilot pull him out and fly him to the next target.

Directly below Bolan was a sparse forest. Under the canopy of cypress boughs, he hoped to find Hasseim's militia. He had trained to jump into trees. The technique required a skillful working of the risers to make his ultradense chute provide enough lift at the final instant for a soft landing.

Keeping an eye on the altimeter LED, Bolan watched the canopy rushing up fast. At three hundred feet, he pulled his rip cord, and the miniature chute on his back deployed with a small pop. He was jerked upward violently enough to rattle his teeth as the superdense nylon weave all but stopped his fall. A few seconds later he felt his feet graze the top of a tree, and he began working the risers. The chute pulled and relaxed like a parasail, assisting his gentle glide into the trees where he settled on a solid limb roughly twenty feet off the ground. Reaching out, he grabbed a nearby branch to get his balance, remaining motionless until he was sure the bough was solid. Once he felt steady, he inched his way to the center where he wedged himself into the crook formed by the branch and trunk.

The Executioner was out of his parachute harness within seconds, tying the straps to a branch so they wouldn't be discovered by anyone who happened to walk by. Drawing his Beretta 93-R, he peered through his night-vision goggles at the ground twenty feet below. The lenses amplified the scarcest amount of ambient light hundreds of times, rendering the landscape almost as bright as an overcast day. Not knowing how close he was to the militia he suspected was holed up in this very section of the wooded hills, he remained perfectly still while he looked and listened. When he was satisfied there was no activity in the vicinity of his tree, he switched the vision system to infrared mode.

The view behind his lenses shimmied for a few seconds while the cathode tubes adjusted to the new data stream. The image quickly jelled, displaying a snowy landscape scattered with the silhouettes of various small animals moving through the underbrush. Bolan touched-checked his gear and slid down the tree, switching the goggles back to night vision when he reached the ground.

"On the ground," he whispered.

The pilot replied with an immediate, "Roger."

Data analyses had put an infrared concentration within one hundred yards of Bolan's spot. He moved swiftly across a small path to a swampy thicket of tall grasses. Knowing he was deep in enemy territory, his strategy was to wait and listen for a few minutes for sentries. If the camp was close, there should be a roving guard. He settled into the middle of a six-foot growth of wild grass and assumed a position he could hold for hours if necessary. Breathing calmly and evenly, he slipped into a type of trance that elevated his auditory senses.

The wait was not long. The Executioner heard three sets of footsteps approaching minutes before they rounded the bend in the beaten path twenty yards away. Sweat dripped from his forehead into tiny rivulets that ran along the seam of his goggles, merging at his temples to become a steady stream running down his cheeks. Gnats and mosquitoes flew in and out of his ears and nostrils, searching for a spot left unprotected by the odorless insect repellant he had applied before getting into the chopper. He ignored the discomfort, remaining motionless in the tall blades save for an occasional slow blink behind the high-tech lenses when the tingling of his sclera told him his eyeballs were becoming too dry to function properly. Only then would he allow his eyelids to close deliberately over each cornea—right one first, then the left—never allowing his task environment to drift, not even for the span of an eye blink, from his sight. Over the years, the combat-proved warrior had learned in unforgiving jungles around the world that minuscule details often spelled the difference between life and death.

As Bolan watched through his night-vision goggles, three militants came into sight. The men were armed with first-class weapons—Heckler & Koch MP-5Ns, one of the smaller variants of the popular submachine gun favored by U.S. Navy special operations units. Designed to accept a clip holding thirty rounds of 9 mm Parabellum ammunition, the personal defense weapon was a formidable piece of hardware.

The men were chatting casually with their guns slung over their shoulders. They passed Bolan's spot without incident, stopping fifteen yards beyond when they reached a clearing in the middle of a thick growth of giant bushes. The men sat on the ground, drank from their canteens and munched energy bars they pulled from their shirt pockets. One went off into the woods, apparently to relieve himself, and Bolan eased slowly from his position to follow.

Gliding silently through the tall lush bushes, Bolan closed in on the man, stopping less than ten feet away when the man unzipped to urinate against the trunk of a gnarled, centuries-old cypress. The night creatures were loud—toads and lizards sang their prehistoric mating songs, punctuated every now and then by the cry of a predator. An irritating undercurrent of insect buzzing rode nonstop on the heavy humidity.

With his Beretta leading, Bolan rushed forward and was upon the man before he had a chance to react. A sharp rap on the back of his skull with the handgun rendered the guy unconscious, and he fell in a heap to the ground. Bolan quickly flipped him over and secured his hands behind his back with a heavy nylon tie wrap he pulled from his web belt. Before returning to confront the others, he removed the gunner's MP-5, tossing it out of sight into the bushes. Pulling the Desert Eagle from its holster, Bolan retraced the man's steps, entering the little clearing at the exact spot where he had walked into the woods. It took a full second for the other two to realize someone other than their partner now stood before them with a weapon in each hand.

"Halt!" Bolan said.

The men probably did not speak English, but in this situation, Bolan knew words were a bit superfluous. They nodded, their eyes glued to the barrels directed at them, and dropped their rifles. With hands interlaced behind their necks, they glared at their captor with murderous intent. Bolan motioned with his weapons, and they dropped to their knees, never taking their eyes off the business end of his pistols.

The Executioner motioned them to get onto their stomachs, and they did as they were told. Once they were both prone, Bolan holstered his Desert Eagle. Keeping his Beretta set for 3-round bursts, he took a step forward while pulling a tie wrap from his web pouch.

One of the men shouted something to his companion and, kicking his legs up, struck Bolan in the knee with his boot. Arching his back, he launched himself from a push-up position straight off the ground as if performing a handstand, finishing his burst upward with a midair half flip that landed him squarely on his feet, facing away.

With his knee buckling inward, Bolan leaned to the rear and squeezed the Beretta's trigger, shooting a 3-round volley into the space between the man's shoulder blades. The 9 mm steel-jacketed slugs hammered him face-first to the ground in a dusty belly flop that could not have been a more dramatic contrast to the gymnastic grace he had displayed moments earlier during his next-to-final move.

The other militant rolled onto his side, grabbing frantically for a combat knife housed in a sheath strapped to the inside of his shin. As his hand closed on the leather-wrapped hilt, Bolan fired the handgun again, drilling a tunnel through his temple. The dead man twitched once before settling onto his back where he lay wide-eyed and unseeing.

Bolan rushed forward to the bodies, concluding after a quick search that there was nothing of strategic value in either man's pockets. With a final glance over his shoulder at the corpses, he walked smartly into the woods, going straight to the unconscious man who lay at the bottom of the cypress with his hands secured behind his back. Bolan lugged him into a sitting position and began to attach the tie wrap, securing his wrists to the tree trunk. He finished just as his prisoner regained consciousness.

The man jerked his head around, locating Bolan. He tugged at the tie holding his hands to the tree, immediately realizing he was out of action. Keeping his captor in view, he started chanting words Bolan recognized as death prayers.

The militant before him believed he was about to die.

After gagging the man, the Executioner turned and walked away, becoming completely engulfed by the thick woods within minutes. Upon reaching the two corpses that were already attracting swarms of flies that droned maddeningly in the night's heat, he took a few moments to throw the MP-5 submachine guns into the woods.

"Two dead, one out," he said softly.

"Roger," came the reply.

As he made his way through the trees on a course perpendicular to the patrol route, he considered his next action. The cybernetics team thought Hasseim would divide his forces, especially if they were equipped with a sizable inventory of missiles. That way, if one location was overrun, the other could continue the attack. With his combat senses on full alert, Bolan considered the various scenarios he and Barbara Price had discussed at Stony Man Farm. They had thought he might find a cave housing up to a hundred militants, agreeing that if he came into contact with a force greater than two dozen, he'd call in the 82nd Airborne. The pilot had them standing by on an alternate frequency—all Bolan had to do was say the word.

There was sound up ahead, and the Executioner lowered himself to the ground, inching forward until he reached the trunk of a thick tree. Peering through the underbrush, he located two militants about fifty yards away, stringing wire up the side of a gently sloping incline. He thumbed a dial on the side of his goggles, framing the men in 15-power magnification. As he watched, they disappeared behind a well-camouflaged stack of sandbags, trailing the wire behind them.

Bolan scanned the area immediately in front of the makeshift bunker, following the wire's direction. Had it not been for his extensive experience deploying the very same weapon, he may not have been able to pick out the crescent moon profile of the Claymore M-18 antipersonnel mine positioned halfway down the hillock.

Taking note of the angle at which the Claymore was aimed, Bolan eased himself away from the tree. To put himself outside the weapon's sixty-degree kill zone, he'd have to traverse about a hundred yards to one side before circling back. The trees on Bolan's left thinned into small groups, creating numerous open pockets where he'd be exposed. Staying low, he moved smoothly to the right, gliding through scrub cypress and wild grasses, quickly putting distance between himself and the two hardmen positioned behind the sandbags.

Claymores, he reasoned, would be deployed as a perimeter defense close to the camp. When he attacked this two-man outpost, he wanted to do it without alerting the others.

He reached a wide, deep gorge running perpendicular to his travel, one of the many scars carved aeons ago into the cradle of human civilization by the retreating ice age. The rocky chasm provided a natural barrier for a small militant camp, protecting one flank of the hillside position as effectively as a twenty-foot chain-link fence topped with concertina wire. Its location told Bolan that the two men with the Claymore were deployed on the camp's outermost boundary. Touch-checking his 93-R to make sure the Beretta's magazine was properly locked, he angled the direction of his approach to bring himself behind their position.

They were facing away, their MP-5s resting within easy reach by their sides. The three on patrol had not been wearing body armor, leading Bolan to assume the same for these men. From a spot less than twenty yards away, he took careful aim. The Beretta coughed twice within a second, its 9 mm rounds delivering instant death as they pierced the militants' hearts.

The Executioner hustled forward to their position,

quickly locating the Claymore's compression trigger, a unit the size of a deck of cards made out of molded plastic. Placing it on top of the sandbags where he'd be able to easily grab it on the way out, he followed the wire, moving downhill to the weapon. Bolan turned the Claymore so that it faced up the slope. He didn't know if he'd use it during his exit, but under no scenario would it do him any good pointed the way it had been.

Bolan approached the camp by going straight back from the sandbags. A well-trained unit would space its security in such a way as to create overlapping arcs. With the gorge to his right, and Claymores designed for sixty-degree coverage, Bolan thought the next security outpost might be about one hundred yards away. He'd circumvent it by heading straight to the center.

The small hillock leveled out in front of a shallow cave tucked into the side of the hill. If the microwave transmitter was in the area, it would be in the cave. From a kneeling position behind a leafy thicket, Bolan scanned the camp through the night vision's magnification. One-man pup tents were pitched in a compact group at the cave's mouth, from which gentle light spilled into the night. Half a dozen men sat outside, speaking in low voices. Shifting his gaze to the cave, Bolan could see from the shadows that it was much too small to house a transmitter the size of the one he had captured in Manitoba. Nevertheless, this was one of the three locations intelligence indicated was dangerous. In order to make sure the device was not there, the site required investigation. He rose to a crouch and dashed from the thicket to a clump of wild olive trees.

The Executioner came under fire as soon as he reached his intended position. Diving to his right where the base of the trees would give him a bit of cover, he pulled the Desert Eagle from his hip holster and returned fire, the .44-caliber weapon's deep-throated roar announcing his location. As a handful of gunners came rushing from the cave to join those outside scrambling for their weapons, Bolan engaged the two who had initiated the firefight. They were shooting from kneeling positions behind adjacent trees, the upper half of their heads visible above the stubby barrel of their MP-5s. Before their comrades could fully join in the fray, Bolan drew his Beretta and pointed it in their direction. With the fire selector dialed to the tight three-dot triangle, he began squeezing the trigger as rapidly as he could.

A 3-round burst found the militant on the right, exploding his forehead into a crimson cloud that stained the tree trunk with a foot-long streak of bloody brain tissue. Without diminishing his steady reply, Bolan shifted his volley to the other gunner, slicing away the thin cypress he had chosen for cover. The bullets walked like army ants across the bark and into the man's face, throwing back the entire top of his head. The tree leaned into the notch carved by the bullets, cracked the way trees do when cut with a chain saw, then snapped free and crashed with a leafy thump to a spot next to the body.

Hot lead zipped through the air as the remaining men trained their weapons in Bolan's direction, hosing the area in front of him with 9 mm slugs from their MP-5s. Bullets impacting the olive tree's base hit with such frequency they sounded like a drumroll to the warrior hugging the earth. Remaining within the natural depression formed by the tree's roots, Bolan eased himself a few inches to the rear as he ejected the empty magazine from his Beretta and rammed a fresh one into the ammo port.

Sneaking a glance around the side of the thick trunks,

he saw a militant sprinting toward a waist-high out-cropping. The Executioner engaged the man with a 3-round burst, stitching a diagonal line across his torso. The militant was lifted off his feet by the force of the steel-jacketed rounds, his lifeless body landing with a heavy crash a few feet from the rocks. Heavy fire from a four-man group near the cave began buzzing through the air above Bolan's head, driving him lower into the depression. Keeping low, he holstered the Desert Eagle and reached into his pouch to grab two M-68 high-explosive grenades.

With a locked-elbow motion imitating the action of a catapult, he lobbed the grenades in rapid succession over his head. A few seconds later, their explosions echoed through the woods, shaking the ground with their con-cussion. A medley of angry shrieks told Bolan his bombs had found their target, and before his enemies could react in kind, he rose to his full height and charged forward with both pistols back in his hands.

An enemy soldier was running in his direction, at-tempting to jam a magazine into the ammo port of his MP-5 at the same time he was trying to level the weapon at the intruder. Bolan fired his Beretta once, and the top half of the militant's head disappeared in an explosion of bone chips and gray matter. The man's momentum carried him forward a few additional steps before his lifeless body toppled forward.

The cave was less than ten yards away, and with both handguns spitting flames to keep the remaining mili-tants behind cover, Bolan pushed forward until he could see the interior. Once he was sure the transmitter was not inside, the Executioner turned back, intent on making an escape down the slope before the men he could hear coming from the hill's other side got there.

His eyes caught the arrival of the first reinforcement, who came onto the scene with his submachine gun eating ammunition on full-auto. He was quickly joined by two comrades, and the mind-chilling sounds of weapons shouting death at their maximum rates of fire increased until it reached an insane volume.

Bolan emptied both magazines as he made his retreat, quickly reloading fresh clips as he sprinted down the hill toward the sandbag bunker inhabited by two dead sentries. When he got close enough, he launched himself into a dive that brought him behind the sandbags as the first of his adversaries came charging into sight, the muzzle-blasts from his rifle illuminating his face.

Behind the protection offered by the sandbags, Bolan returned fire with both handguns. The first man to crest the hillock caught three .44 Magnum slugs in his chest, the heavy bullets spinning him wildly to the leaf-covered ground.

His abrupt appearance was followed by two others, who apparently believed they'd catch their retreating intruder in the open. They paid dearly for their miscalculation as Bolan stitched the first from thigh to shoulder with three rounds from the Desert Eagle. His partner was dispatched a second later with a single round to his head. The hefty slug all but decapitated the soldier.

Springing to his feet, Bolan grabbed the trigger for the Claymore from the top of the sandbags where he had left it earlier. Before additional troops could arrive, he headed down the hill at a full run, trailing the detonation wire behind him. As soon as he passed onto the safe side of the antipersonnel mine, he searched for cover, knowing his pursuers were mere seconds behind.

They were at a disadvantage not knowing how many men they were facing, but with the hardware superiority their MP-5s gave them, it was possible they could overcome their lack of concrete knowledge and experience. There was a slight indentation behind what was probably the oldest tree in the immediate area, its roots forming a gnarly mass at the base of its trunk. Bolan settled into it, holding the Claymore's trigger in one hand, his Desert Eagle in the other.

As he mentally replayed the firefight's first moments, he calculated that he could not be facing more than a dozen enemies. With the three he had encountered on patrol, two in the sandbag bunker and the five he had just shot, he doubted there were more than another dozen. The layout at the cave did not appear to be supporting a greater number than that.

He waited silently, his eyes scanning the lip of the rise. They came into sight within seconds, eight or nine men crawling down the slope so they would not be silhouetted against the background, where they'd be as easy to pick off as mechanical ducks in an arcade.

Bolan swallowed, licked his dry lips and watched them inch closer to the Claymore. From his spot, he had a good view of how the weapon was pointed. He drew mental tangents up the slope from the antipersonnel mine, visualizing the sixty-degree fan, waiting for the lines to contain the approaching enemy. When he pressed the trigger, he wanted to make sure the militants were in a kill zone where there would be less than an inch between projectiles. As still as a statue, he awaited the optimal moment to fire the seven hundred steel balls.

One of his enemies, who had to have been equipped with night vision, spotted him and opened fire, the rounds kicking up dirt and roots inches from his face. Bolan immediately squeezed the Claymore's compression trigger, and the hillside resounded with an incredible detonation that shook the ground as if the very earth had been smitten by Thor's hammer.

With his ears ringing and his head feeling as if it might split, Bolan scanned the slope for survivors. A quick glance told him there was none. From the spot halfway up the hillside where the antipersonnel mine had been positioned to the top of the rise, the ground had been chewed into a honeycomb pattern that extended up the slope in a perfectly defined fan. Bodies lay motionless where they had been caught when the Claymore detonated, their clothes shredded into a bloody paste.

"Not here," Bolan said into his mike. "Let's do two."

"Roger," the pilot replied. "Coming to get you."

The small helicopter swooped into the clearing, hovering for a moment above the sandbags before alighting ten yards from Bolan. He ran to the chopper, jumped in and they were airborne.

"I'm getting real-time intel," the pilot said as they accelerated skyward. "Across the strait. The drones are picking up microwaves. Someone at Bandar-e Lengeh is pinging the frigate below."

"He's sighting it in. Practicing on a real ship in the general area where he's planning to attack the *Reagan*," Bolan said.

The aircraft shimmied under the strain of its full-throttle climb, the blades laboring to cut sufficient air to maintain its forward speed. With the engine screaming at its maximum rpm, Bolan reloaded his handguns, wondering how many caves there were in this region's hillsides. They had selected three sites—what if the transmitter wasn't in any of them? He didn't want to discover its location the hard way when the *Reagan* arrived in a few days.

From thirty-five hundred feet, Bolan could see above

the high grounds to the east where the hint of dawn touched the edge of the horizon. It would start to get light in a few hours, a condition that favored troops defending a fortified position. The Executioner hoped to get in and out before the sun's first rays.

"Approaching LZ," the pilot said over the intercom. "Touchdown in a clearing half a klick from the second objective.

Bolan gathered the rappelling line off the chopper's floor and tossed it out the door. As the pilot made a beeline for the ground, Bolan grabbed the line and slipped outside when they were still a few hundred feet off the ground. He slid down the cord fast enough to make himself a difficult target, reaching the ground mere seconds after exiting the aircraft. Upon touching earth, he spotted a rocky mound roughly three feet high and ran directly for its cover. As the pilot pulled away with the blades noisily chopping air, the Executioner got his bearings.

From the readings on his GPS sensor, Bolan figured he was within a hundred yards of the second cave. There was a steep incline to his front, and at the top of the rise, the objective was cut into the side of the hill. He recalled from enhanced photos taken by passing drones that directly in front of the cave's mouth the hillside leveled off into a flat space twenty yards wide, not unlike what he had found at the first objective. While touch-checking his gear, he switched his night-vision goggles to infrared mode. When the image was stable, he slowly scanned his surroundings.

There was security in place, a fact he hoped was indicative of the value at the top of the hill. Five intersecting laser-thin red lines cut through the space at the foot of the incline, denying direct access. Moving in a crouch, Bolan scampered across the open space to his front, reaching the hillside security where he dropped to one knee behind a scrubby bush. The system was not sophisticated. Five beams coming in a straight line down the hill's slope were set knee-high off the ground. For an intruder without IR sensing equipment, the setup was probably adequate. With his IR goggles, however, Bolan could easily step over the beams, making it all the way to the top without tripping an alarm. If this was the camp's only early-warning system, he might get to within striking distance of the objective before encountering enemy fire.

Moving slowly and deliberately, he began his ascent. He moved quickly up the hillside. A night bird called out, absurdly loud against the peaceful night. Concentrating on his footing lest he slip into one of the beams, he pushed forward.

Behind him, the Strait of Hormuz was about half a mile away. The Navy frigate Bolan and his pilot were using for takeoffs and landings was positioned at the waterway's narrow mouth, looking small from this distance. A deep humming abruptly filled the wooded hillside, increasing in intensity. Remembering the last time he had heard the sound, Bolan immediately identified a microwave transmitter's charging cycle. His hunch that Hasseim was aiming the device for when the *Reagan* arrived was apparently correct. If so, an operator above was about to fire a test beam of microwave at the frigate's conning tower. onboard the ship, Bolan thought the crew would interpret the sudden surge in energy as nothing more than atmospheric lightning.

The Executioner dropped to the ground and assumed a prone position, pulling his posture tight while hugging the earth. The air tingled the way it did before a lightning strike, and an instant later a wave of compressed air smacked his frame, knocking the wind from him. He raised himself to his hands and knees and forced himself to suck in long slow breaths, while he refilled his lungs. By the time the humming wound down and the woods were once again silent, he was ready to resume his approach.

In his left breast pocket he carried a thick plastic bag filled with water and a 6-round clip of orvilles. The explosive rounds offered a significant amount of destructive force, but they had to be used quickly. Once out of the water, the picric acid began drying, initiating a reaction that ended with the creation of an extremely volatile substance. More than one operative had been the victim of a spontaneous explosion when his orvilles dried during the heat of battle.

The Executioner heard them before they saw him. There was a soft clink of metal, perhaps an untapped clip or a rifle's butt plate scraping a rock as the owner moved his weapon, but for a veteran with Bolan's sound management discipline, the three guards sitting together under a trio of olive trees could just as well have used a bullhorn to announce their position. Dropping to one knee, Bolan dialed the magnification knob on his goggles and zoomed in on his enemy's hardware. Two of the men were armed with AK-47 assault rifles. They'd obviously been put on alert after hearing the helicopter.

The Executioner switched his goggles to night vision and began his attack. With his Beretta in one hand and his Desert Eagle in the other, he was prepared to give as good as he got. When he was roughly thirty yards from the trio, he startled a pair of quail that had bedded for the night in his path. The birds frantically beat the air with their wings, crying out their irritation at being disturbed. One of the guards shone a flashlight into the dark, its beam falling directly on Bolan.

A nanosecond after he was discovered, Bolan dived to the right to get out of the light. In midair, he squeezed the Desert Eagle's trigger once, and the throaty roar of the weapon delivered instant death to the man holding the flashlight. The slug blew straight through the guard's gut, exiting at the base of his spine in a hole the size of a baseball. He was dead before his body thudded to the ground.

The night air was suddenly filled with the sounds of AK-47s chattering in full-auto mode as the two remaining guards opened fire. Bullets chewed up clods of earth around Bolan's position as he hugged the ground for all he was worth. Taking a deep breath, he launched himself into a roll moments before a volley of 7.62 mm lead found his position, peppering the spot where he had been an instant before. Using their muzzle-flashes for targets, Bolan fired two shots. His rounds found their mark, and bullets stopped coming from the guards' position.

Reinforcements reacting to the sounds of gunfire appeared across the top of the hillside, some firing their weapons indiscriminately into the night. Bolan assumed a prone position behind an outcropping, hoping they had not seen his muzzle-flashes when he engaged the guards. They apparently had not, because a few began sweeping the area to their front with their assault rifles.

Staying low, Bolan counted the type and number of weapons. There were more AK-47s, Uzis and a smattering of pistols that probably included a few Walthers and Colts. Recalling the microwave test he had noted a short time earlier, he raised his head and peered from behind the rocks. There were at least thirty men at the top of the hill. When they began shining flashlights into the night, Bolan ducked back down.

"Call in the Airborne," Bolan said.

"Roger." There was a short pause. "Done. ETA nine minutes," the pilot said.

The men directly above Bolan began coming down the hillside. With the force of a coiled spring, he jumped to the edge of the rocks giving him cover, exposing half his body as he let loose with a volley from the Desert Eagle. He moved from one target to the next, engaging the militants before they could make any progress down the hill. His enemies scattered in all directions, diving wildly for cover. One of the hefty slugs caught an adversary in midair, twisting his body as the hot lead tore through his hip, shattering his pelvis and lower organs. The man was hammered to the earth where he lay, moaning in agony. A barrage of automatic fire cut the air near Bolan's face. He redirected his Desert Eagle to the shooter, whose face was illuminated by his repeating barrel blasts. Leaning into the rocks for stability, the Executioner zeroed in for a single shot, drilling a fist-sized hole through the man's sternum. He jerked and crumbled into a lifeless heap, going to his death with pistol still in hand.

The rocks were receiving more attention than Bolan wanted, but there was no way for him to dash to a better spot. He fell to a sitting position with his back against the outcropping while in one smooth motion he ejected spent cartridges from his handguns, ramming home fresh ones. Mentally reviewing his opponents' positions, he darted to the edge of his cover and opened fire with both weapons. Enemy rounds sparked and bounced off the rocks, whining with ear-splitting screams as they ricocheted on random tangents into the night sky. There were two men near the base of a tree fifty yards away, and Bolan walked his slugs into their weapons, hearing their cries of anguish as the rounds found their mark. The air surrounding Bolan became a deadly beehive of activity as bullets whizzed by with the distinctive snaps of 7.62 mm ammunition. He pulled back, scrambling to stay as close as he could to the outcropping's back side. On the other side, the automatic fire continued with no sign of ending. Bolan was pinned down and would remain that way until something happened to change the situation.

As he was exchanging the magazines in his handguns for fresh ones, Bolan heard the thud of a grenade landing a short distance up the hill from his location, followed a few seconds later by an explosion that shook the earth. With his guns packing a full load, he edged out from the side of his cover, spotting a man getting ready to throw another grenade. Bolan engaged him as he straightened from a crouch to throw the bomb, hitting him in the chest with a 3-round burst from the Beretta. The man's forward arm motion was halted midthrow, causing him to drop the grenade five or six feet in front of his location. A fellow militant, overcome with panic, jumped up to escape the explosive before it detonated, jumping directly into the Executioner's line of sight. Bolan pulled the trigger on his Desert Eagle at the same moment the grenade went off, the handgun's authoritarian boom lost in the midst of the thunderclap produced by a few pounds of TNT.

His volley was answered with a renewed barrage, as three or four teams of militants hosed the area to the front and sides of the outcropping, spraying a blanket of lead over the area so dense an insect couldn't survive. Bolan hugged the earth, hoping he could maintain the standoff until the Airborne arrived.

He heard the Chinooks and the Black Hawks when they were half a mile away, closing fast on his location. A gunship swooped out of the sky like a prehistoric bird of prey, firing an air-to-surface missile into the side of the hill close to the cave's mouth. The heavy-duty armament threw the militants into disarray as they realized the firefight was being escalated into a full-scale battle. They directed their fire at the incoming helicopters, giving the Executioner enough relief to reenter the fray.

He jumped to his feet and, with both pistols blazing, dashed for a mound of earth that would open a lane up the hillside. As Bolan ran to his new spot, he fired on two guards attempting to engage the approaching troops. His first blast from the Beretta hit the guard on the right inches above his chest. The man fell backward under the force of the Parabellum rounds, his finger freezing in a death grip on the AK-47's trigger. He sent a random spray of bullets into the air, firing in a steady stream until the magazine was spent. His partner received no better, as Bolan's Desert Eagle delivered death from its smoking barrel, sending a serving of hot lead into the man's gut. He stumbled under weak knees into a sitting position, dropped his weapon, and with a low scream that turned quickly into a series of hard grunts, toppled onto his back while clutching his wound in a futile attempt to stem the copious flow of blood that surged warm and steaming into his hands.

The first Black Hawk touched down, bringing with it the chaos of battle. Members of the 82nd Airborne Division leaped from the choppers, immediately launching an assault up the hill. Moving in squad-sized units, they secured the LZ by opening fire on the militants shooting at the arriving helicopters. Within minutes, as more of the division landed, the militants were placed on the defensive. Three American soldiers came running up behind Bolan, and he shouted to them from behind the mound of earth. They covered one another as they advanced, reaching his position where they assumed prone positions. The four began laying down covering fire for an all-out advance.

A whooshing sound filled the air, and a Chinook helicopter exploded midair, victim of a Stinger missile fired from the vicinity of the cave. Secondary explosions twisted and crushed the aircraft as it crashed to earth, becoming a fiery comet of deadly debris. Three more missiles were launched, and another helicopter became a fireball of death.

"Let's go," Bolan said, dashing out from behind the cover. He fired his weapons as he ran up the hillside, engaging targets of opportunity in the midst of the utter confusion and chaos that characterized combat. A muzzle-flash to his left caught his eye, and he directed his weapons on the source, striking a guard who was three steps into a dash for better cover. The Executioner's slugs drilled a neat hole through the gunner's cheek, jerking his head to one side. As his lifeless body flew through the air, his torso twisted in response to his head's motion, crashing to the ground in an awkward pose.

A grenade exploded close by, its concussion knocking Bolan off balance. He was pushed forward hard enough to leave his feet, landing hard against a stretch of gravel. When he scampered to his feet, he felt a stab of pain in his left hamstring. Reaching down, his hand came away bloody, and he realized he had been hit with shrapnel. He sat back down and reached into a pouch on his combat belt for something to bind the wound. From the feel of his muscle, Bolan didn't think the injury was serious, but he wanted to stop the bleeding before it sapped him of his strength. After wrapping his thigh to stem the blood flow, he resumed his advance toward the objective.

Fighting was furious in the flat area at the mouth of the cave. The militants had erected rock barriers they were using for cover as they met the advancing troopers, turning the situation into a standoff. It was only a matter of time before sufficient reinforcements overran the objective, but the militants were prepared to make a fight of it by using their Stinger missiles. As Bolan watched, they fired one after another at the helicopters and soldiers storming the hillside.

From his position twenty yards from the cave, Bolan could see the edge of the microwave transmitter. He turned and grabbed one of the three soldiers who had charged up the hillside with him.

"Cover me!" he shouted above the deafening sounds of battle. Pointing to the cave, he said, "I'm going in there!"

He ejected the magazine from his Desert Eagle and, reaching into his left breast pocket, withdrew the plastic pouch resembling a miniature plasma bag. Slitting it open with his combat knife, he pulled out the wet clip and rammed it into the Desert Eagle's ammo port. With a nod from the soldiers he sprang from his spot and dashed forward, sprinting in short spurts from one depression to another, firing his Beretta as he raced toward the mouth of the cave. He reached it in a final burst of speed as his partner laid down a steady stream of covering lead. Upon reaching the objective, the friendly fire became uncomfortably close, and the Executioner had to watch that he wasn't hit by rounds coming from behind him.

He burst into the cave, a rocky opening that reached about thirty feet into the hill. Two militants directly inside were armed with rifles, but the barrage of incoming rounds had them searching for shelter. Bolan appeared in the mouth, his Beretta spitting death in 3-round volleys. The quick bursts stitched a bloody trail across the two men.

Turning his Desert Eagle toward the microwave transmitter, Bolan was distracted by a man who jumped out from behind the device, holding an Uzi machine pistol in his hands. Bolan fired out of reflex, his mind registering a long jagged scar running down the left side of the militant's face as he pulled the trigger. The Desert Eagle let loose an angry snarl, and the man's head vaporized under the incredible power of an orville round. Bolan was shoved backward by the force, causing him to stumble outside the cave as he leveled his weapon on the transmitter. He fired two orvilles in rapid succession. The shock wave that destroyed the device lifted him completely off his feet and deposited him unceremoniously ten feet away. Upon impact with mother earth, he scrambled to find cover from random rounds zipping through the air.

As he gathered his senses about him, he discovered the source of the Stinger missiles. Ten yards or so from the mouth of the cave, a stockpile of missiles was stacked on pallets. A quick estimate told Bolan there were more than a hundred.

"Plug me into the battle net," Bolan said to his pilot.

There was an audible switch, and Bolan was connected to a voice net extending down to the platoon level.

"Listen up," Bolan said. "Disengage. Disengage. Fire in the hole! Countdown from ten! Ten, nine, eight…" He continued counting as the soldiers retreated, firing to keep the militants at bay.

When he reached zero, Bolan fired his remaining three orvilles as rapidly as he could pull the trigger. The explosive rounds detonated the Stingers they hit, starting a chain reaction that ripped though the missile inventory with a force that blew half the hillside to smithereens. A thunderous explosion pounded his eardrums as an eyeball-searing fireball roared from the stack of Stingers, reaching high into the night sky. The Executioner was blown into the air and thrown twenty feet, landing in the middle of a leafy bush.

When the smoke from the Stinger explosions cleared, he could see that the militants were defeated. Those who had survived the carnage at the top of the hill were being rounded up by the American soldiers, who were herding them into small groups for processing.

The Executioner called for a pickup, and the helicopter swooped out of the sky to take him away from the battlefield.

16

From afar, the crowds jamming the piers of San Diego's Harbor Avenue appeared to be attending a country fair. Red, white and blue helium-filled balloons rose above the crowd, and vendors snaked their way through the throngs, hawking a wide variety of junk food from street carts. Adding to the festive atmosphere, a ninety-piece brass band from the Coronado Navy Yard played patriotic marches from the flight deck of the USS *Midway,* a World War II aircraft carrier that had been converted into a floating museum. The historical ship was dwarfed by the immense USS *Dwight D. Eisenhower,* docked at the adjacent berth. The *Ike* had arrived in port from the Persian Gulf less than one hour previously, and was the object of the welcoming celebration.

Hal Brognola squinted against the glare reflecting off the Bay, and said, "No matter how many times I see that, I'm still impressed."

He was referring to the spectacle of a CVN-class carrier steaming into port with its crew dressed in starched whites, standing at attention along the flight deck's perimeter.

"It's a sight," Bolan agreed.

They were weaving their way through the crowd like two tourists without a care in the world. Bolan walked with a slight limp that favored the tenderness in his hamstring where a piece of shrapnel had been removed upon his return from Iran. The doctors thought he'd be fully recovered in another two weeks.

"We were lucky over there," Brognola said suddenly.

"There's an element of luck in all our missions. One of the things about technology is that it can be used by terrorists to level the playing field. Technology gives aircraft carriers their incredible power, but their very dependence on it also makes them vulnerable. A ragtag militia with no government-sponsored funding almost brought down one of our national assets. It'll only get worse as technology becomes more advanced and available. Those who can influence communications will hold great power."

The big Fed could only agree with that assessment. "I don't like that idea, but you're probably right. The *Ike* will get new software while she's here for servicing, the *Reagan* will gets hers at sea, and the new version will be good only until the next subversive group figures out how to breach security."

A cheer erupted as the first group of crew members came running down the gangplank into the arms of waiting loved ones. Bolan watched as the sailors embraced their wives and children, everyone hugging and kissing. The servicemen grabbed hold of their wives and kids, and cut through the crowd, receiving pats on the back as they made their way toward the parking lots.

A young communications specialist walked past arm in arm with his girlfriend, both chatting nonstop the way young people in love do. The Executioner watched them go by, watching the way the girl kept rubbing her boyfriend's back and hugging his shoulders as if she had to keep touching him to make sure he was really home.

Bolan and Stony Man did what they did to help defend their fellow citizens. It was for moments like this that they lived.

Don Pendleton's Mack Bolan®

The Judas Project

The Cold War just got hot again....

The old Soviet bloc espionage games have resumed on a new playing field: the U.S. financial markets. The enemy isn't the Russian government, but dormant sleeper cells in America's cities, planted by the KGB. Now a former Kremlin official is ready to pocket and manipulate America's resources. He has hijacked operation Black Judas, enlisted the KGB's most lethal assassin and has begun reshaping a plot to steal billions of American dollars. But he didn't plan on a beautiful Russian cop on a vengeance hunt, or an American warrior named Mack Bolan in deadly pursuit, gunning for blood and justice.

Available September wherever books are sold.

ROOM 59

THE HARDEST CHOICES ARE THE MOST PERSONAL....

New recruit Jason Siku is ex-CIA, a cold, calculating agent with black ops skills and a brilliant mind—a loner perfect for deep espionage work. Using his Inuit heritage and a search for his lost family as cover, he tracks intelligence reports of a new Russian Oscar-class submarine capable of reigniting the Cold War. But when Jason discovers weapons smugglers and an idealistic yet dangerous brother he never knew existed, his mission and a secret hope collide with deadly consequences.

Look for

THE ties THAT BIND

by

cliff RYDER

GOLD EAGLE ®

Available October 2008 wherever books are sold.

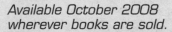

TAKE 'EM FREE

2 action-packed novels plus a mystery bonus

NO RISK
NO OBLIGATION TO BUY